Pra... ...ND

'The characters Michael Farris Smith brings to life might have been f... ...ola, flawed beings with a s... ...e the...

'As viole... as it is poetic, Smi... ... from beginning to end' – P... ...eek...

'Like living languag... ...ry modes ha... ...a formal... a demotic form. W... ...call "noir" is hig... tragedy brought down to the forg... and disavowed – the fallen, who can do little but go on falling. Ours to witness the beauty and power of their fall. With *The Fighter*, cleaving to tradition, Michael Farris Smith brings that tradition brilliantly into the present'
– **James Sallis**

'Smith's great talent here is writing about ancient, universal concerns – parents and children, aging, and place – in a setting so vivid and specific that the book practically tracks mud up onto your doorstep. His vision of the Delta is powerful and lingering' – *New York Journal of Books*

'Equal parts brutal and beautiful and harrowing, it's left me totally bereft' – **Chris Whitaker, Author of** *Tall Oaks* **and** *All The Wicked Girls*

'Smith…excels in this dark and violent South... ...lit thriller. Fans of James Lee Burke will delight... ...ng sense of place in the Deep South, while fans of David Joy will appreciate the protagonist's inner turmoil'
– *The Library Journal*

'Crisply written tale of thwarted lives and rawboned courage'
– *Booklist*

Other books by Michael Farris Smith

Rivers
The Hands of Strangers
Desperation Road

THE FIGHTER
Michael Farris SMITH

HIGH LIFE HIGHLAND LIBRARIES	
38001800395075	
BERTRAMS	01/10/2018
CRI	£7.99
AF	

NO EXIT PRESS

First published in the UK in 2018 by No Exit Press,
an imprint of Oldcastle Books Ltd, PO Box 394,
Harpenden, AL5 1XJ, UK
noexit.co.uk

A CIP catalogue record for this book is available from the British Library.

ISBN
9781-84344-994-2 (B format)
978-1-84344-995-9 (epub)

2 4 6 8 10 9 7 5 3 1

Typeset in 10.8pt Garamond MT with Frutiger Light
by Avocet Typeset, Somerton, Somerset, TA11 6RT
Printed and bound in Great Britain by Clays Ltd, Elcograf S.p.A.

For more information about Crime Fiction go to @crimetimeuk

To be alive at all is to have scars – John Steinbeck

PROLOGUE

When he was two years old the boy was dropped off at the donation door at the Salvation Army secondhand store in Tunica wearing nothing but a sagging diaper. A Planet of the Apes backpack stuffed with more diapers and some shirts and mismatched socks and little green army men was dropped on the ground next to him. Then a hungover woman banged a scabbed fist on the metal door and a hungover man blew the car horn and she ran around and got in as the child watched with a docile expression. Out of the car window the man called out some sort of farewell to the child that was lost in the offbeat chug of the engine and then the foulrunning Cadillac rattled out of the gravel parking lot, leaving the child in the dustcloud of abandonment.

The door opened and two women in matching red Salvation Army t-shirts stared down at the boy. Then they looked into the parking lot at the still lingering cloud. Out into a gray morning sky. They glanced at each other. And then one said I guess we're gonna have to hang a sign next to the one that says no mattresses that says no younguns. The other woman lifted the boy and held him up beneath his arms as if to make certain he was made of actual flesh and bone. When she was satisfied she hugged the child close and rubbed her hand across the back of his head and she said I pity those who have to live behind me in this weary and heartless world.

The police were called and while they waited the women washed the boy in the bathroom sink with paper towels and hand soap. Filthy feet and filthy hands and the diaper was two changes past due. After they had wiped him clean and filled the trash can with dirty paper towels the boy stood naked and fresh on the smooth concrete floor of the bathroom and they admired his innocence and beauty. He was then dressed in a new diaper and a Spider-Man shirt taken from a rack in the kids section. The boy did not cry and did not talk but instead sat satisfied between the women on a tweed sofa marked fifteen dollars as if he had already decided that this was his new home and he was better off.

He was better off but this was the beginning of a childhood spent in the company of strangers. The next ten years saw him move from one Delta town to the next. Four foster homes and two group homes. Five different schools. A handful of caseworkers. Teachers whose names he could not remember and then stopped trying to remember because he knew he would not be in their classrooms for long. The steady and certain build of restlessness and anxiety in this child who was certain neither where he had come from nor where he was going.

When he was twelve years old the assistant director of the group home told him to gather his things. Again. He sat on the bench seat of a white van with the home logo on the side and he watched the fields of soybeans and cornstalks with sullen eyes as he was driven from the sleepy, bricked street town of Greenwood to his fifth foster home. Moving northwest and closer to the great river, to the fringes of Clarksdale, the once bustling Delta hub of trade and commerce that now wore the familiar faded expression of days gone by. His eyes changed when the van pulled into the dirt driveway that led to a two-story home. A white antebellum with a porch stretching across the front on the bottom and top floors. Flaking paint on the sun side and vines hanging in baskets along the porch with their twisted and green trails swaying in the wind. A woman sat in a rocker and she rose to meet them. She wore work gloves and she pulled them off and tossed them on the ground as she approached the van as if readying herself for whatever might be climbing out.

She took him to his upstairs room and opened the dresser drawers to show him where he could put his things and he told her there was no use.

'I won't be here long enough to mess up the covers on the bed.'

'Sure you will,' she answered.

'No I won't,' he said. A twelve-year old certain of the workings of the world.

'Are you gonna run away?'

'I don't know. Are you?'

'Because unless you run away this is where you live now.'

'So you think.'

'So I know,' she said.

'You don't know nothing,' he said and he walked out of the bedroom and down the stairs and out into the backyard. She stood at the window and watched him between the slit in the curtains. He did not stop in the backyard but crossed it and walked out onto the dirt road that ran on and on between the rows of cotton. The sun high and a short shadow followed him. She did not chase. She stood in the window and watched until he was nearly out of sight and she was one step toward the door to run after him when he stopped. A tiny figure in the distance.

He stopped and stayed in the same spot for several more minutes and she could not know that he was talking to himself. Telling himself I don't wanna do this no more. I don't know why I can't have somebody. With the space between them she could not have noticed that he looked back at the big house and said that place right there don't want me neither and that woman can't catch me. I'm gonna take off running and she won't never catch me. Won't nobody. I don't wanna do this shit no more. She could not have heard him or *seen him with any detail but she waited. Only could see that he had stopped. She whispered a prayer without moving her lips as if even the slightest flutter would spook the boy and send him fleeing on furious and reckless feet. He stood still talking to himself and she stood still whispering a quiet and motionless prayer. And then from the distant sky a hawk flew toward the boy. It flew low and its wings were spread wide and when it reached the vicinity of the boy it swooped and seemed to hold there out in front of him. Begging the boy to admire its eloquence. Begging the boy to notice something other than himself and his troubles. Begging the boy to think of something other than running from that woman. The hawk rose and fell again and the boy saw it and his eyes followed the hawk as it turned long and graceful curves in the bluewhite sky. From the window Maryann spied the hawk and she shifted her eyes from sky to land, waiting to see what the boy would do. The breath she had been holding was let go when the hawk turned toward the house. And the boy followed.*

Round One

1

HE PASSED THROUGH VICKSBURG AT MIDNIGHT, the dull lights of the nonstop convenience stores and fast food restaurants fading in the rearview mirror as he drove onto Highway 61 and made his way north and into the Delta. The great alluvial plain spanning for thousands of acres, centuries of flooding from the Mississippi River creating deposits of the most fertile soil in the world, soil that for generations had made many rich and many more poor. Hundreds of flat miles. Haunts of slaves and soldiers. A land of the forgotten covered by boundless skies.

Between his legs a pint of Wild Turkey. Between his fingers a skinny, woodtip cigar. In the cupholder a gas station cup of coffee. On the passenger seat an open plastic bag with two dozen red pills that killed the pain. His eyes scattered and alive and his cigar hand tapping the steering wheel to the stiff metal beat from the radio and the thumpity thump of the uneven highway. Halfwired, halfdrunk, fully loaded. There were few other headlights and out on the empty highway he floated from his lane and into the other and back again as if the truck itself was bored with the night.

On the seat next to the bag of pills was an open box of the woodtip cigars, a pile of shirts and jeans, the belt he had taken off as he hurried across the parking lot of the casino in Natchez a couple of hours before. Getting to the truck and opening the door, removing his belt and tossing it inside and shoving the envelope of cash into the glovebox and driving away before anyone found the man he left lying facedown on the bathroom floor.

The truck seat and floor were littered with shiny cartridges to a pistol he no longer owned and crumpled pawnshop receipts and a spiral notebook filled with dates and names and notes he had written to himself. By each name he had written friend or foe. By each address he had written safe or stay away. The pages were filled with fragments of directions and phone numbers and what he owed and who he owed it to and other notes he had written out of frustration or anger or despair, notes to remind him of which world he belonged to. Two pages were committed to Maryann and only Maryann, halfsentences about her deterioration and when he had last seen her. Tucked behind the pages for Maryann was the folded foreclosure notice and across the top of the notice were checkmarks to keep track of the days because the clock was ticking. He had looked at the notice before he drove out of the casino parking lot and he had been gone from Clarksdale for twenty-two days. Eight left before the notice of sale would be delivered. He was not yet so detached from his own memory to need every note and name and warning but he was preparing for that day to arrive as chunks of his past had disappeared and little by little the recent had begun to flake away as if skinned with a sharp and shiny blade.

He smoked the cigar to the tip and then let down the window and the night air whipped and momentarily chased the squalid smell out of the truck cab. He tossed the cigar butt and an orange trail of sparks danced and disappeared into the night. He drank from the Wild Turkey and drove a little faster. Drank from the coffee cup and turned down the radio. A pinch in his shoulder as he reached for the dial. A grip in his lower back as he situated in the seat. The clock read 12:27 and he tried to remember how long it had been since the last pill and he reached over into the plastic bag and took a tiny red one. He popped it into his mouth and chased it with the bourbon and reared back his head and stretched his neck and his eyes watered as the pill and liquor went down hot. The wind was strong in the window and he leaned out and spit and then rolled it up. Opened the glovebox and took out the envelope to make sure it was still there. That he hadn't imagined it.

It was a folded manila envelope with the Magnolia Bluffs Casino logo in the top left corner. A sprawling magnolia flower that spoke more of debutantes than roulette. He steadied the steering wheel with his knees and opened the envelope and took out two stacks of cash, five grand each. A rubber band held a smaller stack of bills and he looked at the three stacks, smelled them, stuck them back into the envelope. He took out the note he had written to himself – 12K straight to Big Momma Sweet. He stuck the note in the front pocket of his jeans and the envelope into the glovebox and then he took out the photograph of the woman and child.

He flipped on the light in the truck cab and looked at himself and Maryann as they stood in front of his first car. A boy of sixteen with his shirt off and brown from the sun. Her kneehigh skirt and sandals and her hair dirty blond but beginning to show silver streaks and each with a hand propped on top of the hatchback. Rusted bumper and the hood a different color from the rest of the car but bought and paid for. Still a year before he stepped into the cage for the first time. Another twenty years before her mind betrayed her to the point of being a risk to herself. Still time for us both to be saved, he thought.

His life was filled with drug dealers and illegal gamblers and men who killed dogs with other dogs and fighters like himself who lived in violent and unforgiving worlds. There had been women and even when he had found a small sympathy or something tender he knew that it was not true but part of the trade. The only one who loved him was sitting in a nursing home in Clarksdale and could no longer recognize his face or his name and he had betrayed her beyond even his own imagination but he had eight days to bring her home.

He turned the photograph over. In recent ink he had written ME AND MARYANN. He brushed a thumb across the words and then set the photograph on top of the casino envelope. Turned off the light. For three weeks he had crossed the Mississippi River back and forth between Natchez and Vidalia. Hiding out in a motel room in Vidalia and driving over the bridge and to the casino when he had enough cash to play. Getting hot and going cold and then going to the abandoned sawmill on the outskirts of Vidalia when he was flat busted, where the moon stared down upon the empty land and they fought on Friday and Saturday nights. Getting on the card and doing what he could to survive another night of fists and knees, doping himself into slow motion to keep the crippling headache at bay while the knuckles went into his ribs or the side of his neck. Managing to stay upright long enough to get paid and then going to the motel room. Running the bathtub full of hot water and then settling his tired body into the water and his head back against the tub and his eyes closed and waiting. Waiting for the moment when he could rise again. Take the two hundred dollars they had given him for the fight over to the casino and this time would be the time. All you need is sixty great minutes, he told himself. And you can pay Big Momma Sweet and then you can pay the man at the bank and go and get Maryann and no more fighting and no more of this other shit and you can sit with her where she belongs, move her bed out to the porch and watch the sun cross the sky and the shadows shift and just be there with each another.

But they were on him. Someone had seen him at the fights in Vidalia and knew he owed Big Momma Sweet and that someone made a call and then they came. A price on his head. He had headbutted one in the alley behind the motel and knocked another unconscious in the casino bathroom after he had a big run. He had to get back to Maryann and he had to clear himself with Big Momma Sweet or else they would find him and hurt him. So he had stepped across the man on the bathroom floor, the blood coming from his nose and puddling on the glossy tile and he hustled to the cashier and emptied his pockets that were full of one hundred and five hundred dollar chips and he had just enough to get clear with her and a few hundred left over to get him started at the next casino. He believed in the miracle of getting hot one more time, just one more time, without her goons looking over his shoulder. With nothing to do but get to thirty thousand and rip the foreclosure notice into shreds and take Maryann out of that place.

He was hellbent toward the Delta now, going to see Big Momma Sweet way out there in that deadend spot of the world where the river was wide and black and where the old graveyards wrestled to keep the dead in their graves and where a man vanished if he didn't pay what he owed. Deliver, he told himself. Deliver and then fill the canyon you have dug for yourself with rocks and dirt and then cover it with sod and plant flowers and trees and if somebody walks by they'll never know how deep and cavernous and jagged was the canyon.

He punched the truck ceiling and let out a quick, vicious

scream. He'd had the chance to score it all, the twelve thousand for Big Momma already in his pocket and as he walked into the casino bathroom he knew all he needed was two more sets of kind cards at the blackjack table. He would go and sit back down and bet it all and get to twenty-four. Bet it all again and get to forty-eight and without looking at the dealer again or the waitress again and without listening to the gasps and cheers from those who would be standing around the table he would simply gather the chips and walk to the cashier. Drive back to Clarksdale and when the sun came up the house would belong to her and not the bank. His life would belong to him and not to Big Momma Sweet. He punched the truck ceiling in quick thrusts, knowing he should have never gotten up and gone to the bathroom. Knowing he should have sat still at the table with the fresh ice in the drinks, with the bullshit smiles from the dealer. With the smooth, green felt of the tables, with the fake red leather cushions of the table chairs. Knew he should have stayed there while his blood was running right and while the cards laid down like he needed them to and while the woman across the table was leaning forward in her lowcut dress and telling him with the flap of her long lashes, I'm yours if you want me. Stay hot, baby. Stay hot.

But instead he was driving through the night. The dangerous debt in the glove box. The miracle still on hold. This midnight concoction of caffeine and nicotine and bourbon and the sweet little pills for the busted parts of his body. It all kept him running so that he could get back into the black land where he could walk into the ramshackle cabin where they played for blood and sometimes more and say to Big Momma Sweet here you go and toss the envelope into her broad, cushy lap. Here you go and if one of your boys follows me out of here and comes my way in some parking lot or sits down across from me anywhere

I'll break him in half and bury the top part and send you the bottom part so you can kiss his dead ass.

He wiped his forehead with the back of his hand. Looked at himself in the rearview mirror. Short brown hair, gray filtering in above his ears. Long sideburns that hid a jagged scar that ran from his earlobe and along the jawline of the left side of his face. A crooked nose. Scar slices across his forehead. Jack Boucher, he whispered and he shook his head. You ain't nothing but a broken down dirty dog. Then he said his name louder, dragging out each syllable. *Boo-shay. Boo-shay.* Remembering Maryann teaching him how to say it. Almost thirteen years old and hearing his name pronounced correctly for the first time. She listened to him repeat it and then she interrupted and said do you know what it means in French?

Le Boucher, he said to himself in the rearview mirror. The butcher.

He rubbed at his temple and shifted in the seat and with each move he felt it. He felt the twenty years of granite fists and gnarled knuckles beating against his temples and the bridge of his nose and across his forehead and into the back of his head. The sharp points of elbows into his kidneys and into the hard muscles of his thighs and into his throat and the thrust of knees against his own and into his lower back and against his ears and jaw. He felt the twist of arms and legs and wrists and ankles, being turned and wrenched in ways that God didn't intend for them to be turned and wrenched. He felt the breaking of his own teeth and the blood in his mouth and the swollen fingers and swollen eyes and the ringing in his ears and the chainlink fence mashed against his face. He felt the scars and slit in his tongue and the small knots across his body that had risen but never fully disappeared and he felt the rust in his joints when he wiggled his fingers or turned his head or raised his arms to pull on a shirt. The crash of his body against the hard floor and against any of the four steel poles of the cage corners. He felt the pain in his head from concussion after concussion after concussion after concussion and he lived in the blurred world of a rocked mind. He felt the streaks of pain through his eyes and down his spine and he felt the burst of bright lights and the sharp, unexpected noises of the modern world that screamed through his brain. Broken fingers and dislocated kneecaps and sprained neck and gashed skull and again and again and again the fists and knuckles and knees and elbows and he felt it all as if every blow he had absorbed and every blow he had delivered still existed somewhere in an invisible cloud of pain that draped and held him like some migrant soul in search of home. The years passing and his body rusting and his mind like some great wide open space with howling and twisting winds and swirls of memory that could not differentiate between now and then and he felt it all.

He drove north and the earth flattened and the night opened up her wide, welcoming mouth and took him in. Stay awake, he thought. Stay hot. Rumble through the dark with abandon.

2

To the west heat lightning struck against the eternal horizon and provided his drunk and doped eyes with something to chase as he drove on between the low black fields. It had been a hard summer and headhigh metal sprinklers stood tall in the cotton and soybean crops and worked through the relief of night, shooting widereaching sprays out across the thirsty land. Bugs raced past in the headlights and he crushed an armadillo or possum and he yelled for the truck to get on up as he goaded the engine like he was pushing a hardworn horse across a hardworn land.

He was only a dozen miles from Clarksdale when he had to stop for gas at an allnight store in Alligator where they smoked ribs day and night in black steel drums. It was a cinderblock building with a crooked aluminum awning covering the single gas pump. From behind the building the smoke wafted up and into the night and after Jack put gas in the truck he let his hunger guide him around behind the store where a huddle of old black men sat in folding chairs and drank tallboys. On a table beside them were three packs of cigarettes and a gallon milk jug filled with homemade barbecue sauce. A stack of wood and halfbags of charcoal stacked beside the smokers.

The back door of the store was open. Inside half a dozen people sat on milk crates and a ratty loveseat in front of the beer coolers and in front of them a duo played. The thump of a kickdrum and the shrill of a harmonica kept the knees of the nocturnals bouncing.

Jack approached the men sitting outside and asked who he needed to pay for the gas.

"'I'll take your money, honey," said a graybeard. He put his hand on the shoulder of the man next to him and pushed himself up. "How much you get?'"

Jack held out a twenty dollar bill. 'All that.'

'Good cause I ain't got no change.'

'In my whole life of stopping at this store y'all never have.'

'Whole life? I ain't never seen you,' the graybeard said.

'I come and go.'

The graybeard turned to the other old men. 'Y'all know this boy?'

All shook their heads but one. He wore a straw hat cocked on his head and he got up and moved close to Jack. 'Yep,' he said. 'He's that boy that cost me all that damn money over in Itta Bena one night.'

The huddle laughed and one of them said 'What the hell you doing in Itta Bena anyhow?'

'Losing my damn money on this old boy. Way out in the damn sticks in this dirt pit where shouldn't damn nobody be. Like to got my ass carried off by mosquitoes. And got my pockets holed out.'

'Holed out because I won or lost?' Jack asked.

'Don't recall.'

'Because if you lost when I won then you should've known better.'

'You don't look like you never won much of nothing,' the

man in the straw hat said and he craned his neck to get a better look at Jack's scarred and crooked face.

'You got anything to eat?' Jack said.

'Not for you,' said the man in the hat.

'Naw. Come on now,' the graybeard said. 'If you gonna bet, you got to be a man if you lose it. Cause your snakebit ass damn sure knows you gonna lose it.'

The others nodded and said you know that's right. That's right.

The graybeard grabbed a halfrack of ribs wrapped in tin foil from the table. He held it out to Jack and Jack reached for it but staggered.

'Shit,' said the graybeard. 'You need to sit your ass down.'

Jack got his hand on the ribs and the man held tight. And then he reached in his pocket and pulled out a crumpled ten and handed it to the old man.

'You better sit down,' he said again.

'I'm all right.'

'Sit down and eat them ribs. Sly over there'll give you one of his beers.'

'Say what?' Sly said.

'Y'all quit being so damn greedy.'

Inside, the kickdrum and harmonica stopped. Jack walked over and leaned against the table and began to unfold the tin foil. The graybeard told Sly to give the boy a beer and he reached into a cooler and set a tallboy on the table next to Jack. He ate and drank while the men went back to jawing about the mean women they had loved and the hot ass sun that made them that way.

In the doorway of the store the harmonica player lit a cigarette. He was skinny and taut and wore a t-shirt with the sleeves and neckline cut off. He watched Jack and smoked his cigarette and then slid the harmonica into his pocket. His teeth were gray and scraggly hairs dripped from his chin. He watched Jack slurp the beer and gnaw at the ribs and he slid back inside. He picked up the telephone and dialed. It was the middle of the night but he knew she would want to know what he was looking at. And if he could deliver what he was looking at then he could save his own skin that Big Momma Sweet had threatened to peel off his back.

A deep voice answered.

'She up?' Skelly said.

'Who is this?'

'Does that make a difference whether or not she's up?'

'Yep. It do.'

'Then it's Skelly.'

'She ain't up.'

'Hell just hold on. She might be up for what I see about twenty yards from me.'

'She don't care.'

'Jack Boucher,' Skelly said with a tone of finality and triumph.

A long pause came from the other end of the line.

'You hear me?' he asked after waiting. Then through the doorway he saw Jack kill the beer and wipe his mouth on his shirtsleeve. He bummed a cigarette and then nodded to the men and headed for the truck.

'I ain't got time for this. You want him or not?'

'Bring him here.'

'Not without a damn promise.'

'Promise what?'

'That I don't owe shit.'

'She says no.'

'You didn't ask her.'

'I don't have to.'

'You better think good and hard again cause he's walking toward his truck right now. I get him there and I don't owe nothing to nobody.'

Another pause. Outside the truck cranked.

'You get him here and you don't owe nothing to nobody,' the deep voice answered and then a click.

Skelly dropped the phone and snatched a pack of cigarettes from behind the store counter. The drummer was coming out of the bathroom and asked where Skelly was going but he didn't answer. He hustled out of the building and was standing in front of the truck when Jack turned on the headlights.

3

For a long moment they stared at one another. Jack's face dark inside the cab and Skelly squinting in the headlights but they stared and waited on the other to say the first word. Skelly held his open palms out to his side as if to submit. Trying to kill another minute to figure out how to get Jack to let him in the truck. Trying to figure out how to get him out to Big Momma Sweet's place. Trying to remember if he'd ever crossed Jack and hoping he wouldn't simply put the truck in drive and run him over.

Jack waved him out of the way.

Skelly put his hands on the hood and yelled wait a second.

Jack revved the engine and Skelly moved to Jack's open window, his hands held back as if to avoid something that might scald.

'Hold on now. Haul me into town if it ain't a bother. I just need a ride on up to Clarksdale if you're going that way.'

Jack looked him up and down. Sweaty from blowing and sucking on the harmonica and a sunkback jaw that Jack had seen many times before in the faces of the walking dead who tried to trade him meth for pills.

Skelly figured Jack would have known him by now without the dirty windshield between them. They had sat together in poker games and Skelly had fought on the same card as Jack a few times down in Greenville. Way back when Jack was a main event. And they had smoked and turned up whiskey bottles afterward. Skelly raised his hands above his head and was about to say his name when Jack interrupted.

'What you want again?'

'Just a ride.'

'Why you got your hands up?'

Skelly lowered them. Thought to say do you remember me but he could tell by the vacant stare that Jack had no idea of who he was.

'Just on up a little ways. My old lady stays in that trailer park right before town.'

'Nah,' Jack said.

'Come on, man. I'm already in deep shit. I got to get home.'

'That ain't my problem.'

Skelly pulled some wadded bills from his pocket and said I can pay you.

Jack leaned his head out the window. 'What you got?'

Skelly flattened and counted the money. 'Seventeen,' he said. 'And you can have it all.' He extended the money to Jack.

'Where you going again?'

'Just right up the road.'

'What's your name?'

'What?' Skelly said.

'Your name. What is it?'

Skelly looked past Jack and an empty pack of cigarettes sat atop the gas pump. 'Kool,' he said.

'Your name is Cool?'

'Yeah. With a K.'

'Like the damn cigarettes?'

'My momma loved them so.'

'Sounds to me like she loved way worse than that,' Jack said. He opened the notebook and looked for the name Kool in his list of enemies. When he didn't see it he closed the notebook and dropped it behind the seat. Then he told him to get in.

Skelly hadn't even closed the door behind him when he pointed at the pint of Wild Turkey and asked for a drink. Jack nodded and Skelly gave him a cigarette in return. Jack eased out onto the highway and they rode for several silent miles. After a few sips from the bottle Skelly said it'd be fine with me if we kept on riding a little while. My old lady ain't exactly interested in seeing me no way.

'What'd you do?' Jack asked.

'Nothing. Just can't keep her happy. You know how they are.'

'Not really.'

'You ain't got an old lady?'

Jack shook his head.

'Cause we can keep riding. I know this place out close to the river that don't never stop.'

'So do I.'

'We can go on out there. My old lady's mad anyhow.'

'You already said that.'

'Well. She is.'

'I told you I'd take you to your trailer park. Nowhere else.'

Skelly drank from the bottle again and waited. Waited for Jack to place him. Waited for Jack to remember that his name was not Kool. Waited for those hard eyes. But he kept waiting and riding and nothing. He drank again and passed the bottle over. Jack drank and then screwed on the cap and set it on the seat. Then Skelly opened the glovebox.

Jack reached over and slammed it shut. He thrust his forearm against Skelly's throat and pinned his head against the headrest.

'Keep your damn hands to yourself,' Jack said.

Skelly couldn't answer and he slapped at Jack's forearm to get some air. Jack held him until Skelly's tongue came out and then he lowered his arm. Said if you wanna start walking across this black night with a broken nose or worse then do that shit again.

Skelly coughed and tried to get his breath. 'Damn it. You ain't got to do all that.'

'Not one thing in here belongs to you. You got it?'

'I got it.'

'Sit fucking still and ride. First lights I see and your feet hit the ground.'

And then the knife came out. Jack never saw it but he heard it snap open and then felt it against his throat.

'You son of a bitch,' Skelly said. 'Don't look like you're the boss no more. You'll do what the hell I say and you'll take me where I want to go.'

Jack nodded a little. Let off the gas.

'Don't even slow down,' Skelly said and he took the dangling cigarette from his mouth. 'You gonna go out to the river. Out where I say. Or I'll open you like a tuna can.'

Jack nodded again. Drove on through the unresolved night with a blade on his throat and the sour and smoky smell of this man in his nose. Skelly slid closer to Jack for better leverage with the knife and he caught himself in the rearview mirror. An expression of pride flashed back at him and he believed that this was his night and only his night and it's about goddamn time. Son of a bitch ain't so tough with his nuts shriveled up. Don't nobody put his damn hands on me. Don't nobody. This is my night and he don't know half the shit he's got coming. He smoked and winked at himself in the mirror. My night you son of a bitch. He doublechecked the blade against Jack's throat and then he reached over and opened the glovebox again. Said you done gone and sparked my interest. I wonder just what you got in here now after all that ridiculousness.

Skelly saw the bulk of the envelope and the name of the casino in the left corner. The certainty he had felt from what destiny had already laid at his feet on this humid night when all he had set out to do was to play a little harmonica and get a little drunk now multiplied itself into realms of satisfaction that were foreign to him. The very brief thought flashed in his shallow and eroded mind – I have it all.

He lifted out the envelope and his dull gray teeth showed themselves in the dull black night and in his revelry he did not notice that Jack had gradually been speeding up the truck. Easing from sixty to seventy and now almost eighty with the lightning closer as Skelly turned the envelope in his hand and the bigger he grinned the harder he pressed the knife against Jack's throat and the closer the skin came to splitting and the faster Jack drove. The rhythm of the road thumping quicker beneath the tires and the wind coming harder through the windows and the lightning in front of them in white hot flashes and Skelly began to fumble with the envelope with the one hand. Jack felt either sweat or blood trickle down his neck and he wasn't going to wait to find out which it might be and going almost ninety now he yanked the truck to the left. The knife came off his throat just enough for him to snatch Skelly's wrist and slam it into the dashboard. The knife fell from his hand and Jack let go of the wheel and with both hands he twisted the skinny wrist and it popped like a stick and Skelly howled. The truck swerved off the highway and Jack had to let go of Skelly and wrestle the steering wheel to keep from losing all control. Skelly yelled out in pain as he dropped the envelope and went for Jack's eyes with his good hand. Ninety miles an hour and two men clawing and beating at each other and the truck bouncing and swerving and Jack stomped the brake just as somebody's elbow brought the steering wheel down hard to the right and the truck jerked off the road. It flipped once and then stuck on its side and slid across the fertile ground like some strange metal plow preparing the earth for seed.

4

When Jack came to, the truck rested on its side and the headlights shot out across the rows of cotton. The engine still running and the front wheels spinning and static from the radio. His back was against the passenger side door and his feet were straight up and touched the steering wheel. His shirt was wet and he thought blood but he touched his fingers to the dampness and then to his nose and smelled only whiskey and coffee.

He twisted and turned and managed to get his feet below him and he turned off the ignition. A searing pain shot behind his eyes and he doubled over and went back down, grabbing at the sides of his head. He held his head until the pain let off enough to open his eyes. He felt a knot on his forehead and then he touched the pocket of his jeans. The lighter was there and he pulled it out and flicked it and in the faint light of the flame he looked around his feet for the bag of pills. Or any pill. He reached down with frantic fingertips and then he touched plastic and lifted the bag and a handful of pills remained. A hissing sound came from the engine and he pushed himself up and climbed out of the open driver side window. He sat with his ass on top of the door and he lifted his legs out, swung them around and jumped off and then he fell facedown into the black earth and the pain shot through his head and eyes again like an electrical storm. He screamed into the dirt, his eyes watering and a little blood dribbling from his nose and his body wrenching with the pain.

And then he felt the hand on his shoulder and the gentle voice saying lie still.

So he listened and he lay still. Closed his eyes and face in the dirt and his hands again holding the sides of his head and his mind twisting and turning frantically, trying to situate himself in the right now. Where am I and how did I get here and what the hell am I doing and what is this hand on my shoulder and my God stop this pain and my God my eyes are on fire and calm down calm down calm down and my God stop this pain. He then began to writhe in the dirt as if burrowing into a safer place and again he felt the hand and heard the voice. Lie still, Jack. It will ease if you lie still.

He breathed. Straightened his body and tried to calm. The hand on his shoulder. He breathed and didn't move and the night held him and the pain gradually subsided. The burning diminished. Enough for him to lift his face from the earth and slowly shift to a sitting position. He lifted his shirt and wiped the spit and blood and dirt from his face. The world came into focus and he followed the trail of light across the cottonfilled acres, bugs jetting across the white beams, perfectly planted rows running on and on and on as if an extension into eternity. The truck on its side and a lazy cloud of smoke hovering around the sideways engine.

Come on, she said and she put her hands under his arms and helped to lift him to his feet.

She asked if he could walk and he mumbled and nodded and brushed the dirt from his shirt and jeans. He then looked at her and she was almost as tall as him and her hair was long and white and it seemed to gather the moonlight. She wore a sleeveless dress that bared pale shoulders and arms. He wiped his nose again and doubled over and when he raised his head there was the scent of mint in the breeze and he could only guess that it somehow came with her. She held out her hand and he took it and they began to move along gingerly.

'The truck,' he said.

'It'll be here,' she answered.

'Where are we going?'

'Up ahead. Another mile or so there's a place that's always open. I will get you there and sit you down. The light of day will be here in a few hours and then you'll be able to see what to do.'

His breaths were offbeat, small huffs and catches and he seemed on the verge of crumbling and crying. Don't worry, she said. I have you.

They ambled along the side of the straight, worn road. He crept and she held his arm and talked of the night and the stars and the clumps of cotton that seemed like tiny pieces of moon that had flaked away and fallen to the earth. Nothing moved in the night but for them. Nothing but the two stragglers and their black shapes shuffling through the vacancy.

She whispered to him now, so low that he couldn't make out what she was saying but only that she was whispering and the gentle touches of her voice helped him push on. He hurt all over but he was accustomed to hurting all over and he only wanted to capture her whispers and keep them somewhere inside and he wanted to talk but didn't know what to say and he gathered his strength and fought the pain and he wanted to turn to her and hold her still and get close and see her face and her eyes and tell her of the power of her whispers.

He paused and said hold on. He bent over with his hands on

his knees and he tried to vomit but nothing came out and he dropped to a knee and said I'm sorry. I'm sorry.

She leaned close to his ear and said it's all right and she stroked the back of his head with her hand like a mother tending a sick and sleepy child.

You'll be okay, she whispered.

He put his hands out and caught himself falling and he rested on all fours. He closed his eyes. Didn't know how to answer but he felt the comfort in her being there.

But when he opened his eyes again he was not on the side of the road. And she was not there. He was sitting on a barstool, his weight forward against the bar. A beer can in front of him and a bloody wad of paper towels in his hand and the neon beer sign behind the bar throwing hot red darts into the tender corners of his eyes.

5

THE CARAVAN DROVE ACROSS THE NIGHT in a stretching trail of trucks and trailers and campers. Some towed carnival tents that housed the games and merchandise and others towed carnival rides that spun screaming children around and around in fast and rickety circles. Missing headlights and taillights gave the line a gaptoothed stare into the Delta dark and carnival workers drove and smoked while others slept with their heads propped on folded pillows that pushed against door windows. For the last month it had been shooed by Louisiana lawmen from one abandoned parking lot to the next in towns like Shreveport and Monroe, the long list of citations disappearing in exchange for cash and the promise to pack up and move on. The same story everywhere. The caravan finding empty asphalt in a forgotten part of town and unhooking and having the carnival up and running in a matter of hours. The magic of something having appeared where there had been nothing the day before enough to seduce mommas and children and bored teenagers who approached tentatively, wary of the rough look of the carnival workers and the bang and clack of the rides but who always took out their money and played along.

A twenty-year-old Suburban led the caravan and towed the

red and white striped ticket stand strapped to a flatbed trailer. And the man who led the carnival drove the Suburban with the headlights on bright and he traced his eyes across the emptiness as if expecting some type of ambush or maybe a glimpse of the supernatural. He wore a bandana tied around his neck and a long gray goatee reached to the base of the bandana. An ageless ponytail he wore in a braid fell in front of his shoulder and stretched across his round belly. Rough hands tapped each side of the steering wheel as he hummed a song he could not name and he knew from many years and many miles that Clarksdale was coming soon.

In the distance he spotted the taillights of a truck off to the side of the road against the backdrop of black. Taillights up and down and not side to side. He let off the gas and picked the CB receiver from its hook. Clicked a button and said I'm slowing down. There's something up here. Closer and closer and then he spoke into the receiver again and said everybody pull over and stay right where you are. Don't nobody get out. He eased the Suburban to the roadside a dozen yards away from the wrecked truck and the caravan did as instructed. The vehicles covered a quarter mile and sat still with rough idling engines.

He got out of the Suburban. Hiked his pants up. Opened the door to the backseat and took out a flashlight. He was broad with thick shoulders that time had slowly brought forward and as he lurched toward the truck the headlights of the Suburban gave him a menacing shadow. He looked down at the burrowed earth where the truck had slid. At the back end of the pickup the tailgate had fallen open and was bent and dug into the ground and then he moved to the engine. Drips and a hissing and he sniffed for gas but didn't smell any.

At the front of the truck he saw the splintered windshield. Shined the flashlight into the cab and looked for the body or bodies but there weren't any. He turned from the truck and looked off into the night as if to readjust his eyes and then looked into the truck cab again. Scattered clothes and a whiskey bottle and a knife. But no body. He pulled at his goatee and thought a minute and then he heard the moan.

He backed away from the truck. Listened. It came again. A long moan and then a gurgle. He followed the sound which led him back in the direction of the caravan. A hollow and painful calling in the night and then in the beam of the flashlight he saw the twisted body lying at the bottom of the slope from the asphalt to the cotton. Out of his headlights. Right about where the truck began its slide.

In his nomadic life he had come upon many car wrecks and seen many bodies but this was the first time that he had seen something so skinny and broken. But still the voice called and made incoherent pleas for what he thought could only be death and he untied the bandana from his neck. The arms snapped and legs bent behind and hips shifted and the bloodied face calling for what had to be mercy or forgiveness and he knelt in the dirt and his great shadow fell over the crippled body. And then with his coarse and callused hand he covered the face with the bandana and pinched the bloody nose and covered the open and pleading mouth and only an instant of life remained. Only one more sound came from the man. Not of anguish and pain but instead a falling exhaustion of revelation that there would be no more to this world and soon the breath was gone and the body fell silent.

Baron stood. Folded the bandana and tucked it in his pocket. Hoped that he had given peace. He stared and wondered if there might be another and he shined the light around but only saw earth and crops and then he was interrupted when she crossed in front of the headlights of the Suburban and walked in his direction. He looked up and said I told you to stay where you were.

'I can't help it,' she said. 'I saw him laying there before you did.'

'Then why didn't you warn me?'

'Because you told me to stay where I was.'

'Go get me something to wipe my hands with. I don't think the bandana did it.'

She pulled a handful of napkins from the pocket of her cutoffs and said I figured you might say that.

A door opened and closed from somewhere along the caravan and Baron yelled for everybody to stay your damn ass where I told you to and then he told Annette to get on the walkie and repeat what he just said.

He wiped his hands and stuck the wad of napkins into his pocket with the bandana. Then he meandered the scene again. Looking and listening for anyone else who might be there and he wandered out of the lights and down into the edge of the crop and then to where the skid began but there was nothing to find. Nothing to hear but the hum of engines. Annette returned and leaned on the Suburban with her arms folded. Her body was covered in tattoos and in the shine of the headlights she stood like some black and blue statue.

He stood next to her and shined the light on the truck again. 'I used to have an old gray Chevy right about like that one,' he said. 'And I wrecked it. Like that one.'

'Is he dead, Baron?' she asked.

'Yeah,' he said and he lowered the flashlight.

'What are you gonna do?'

'I already done it. There wasn't no choice. Don't go look.'

'I don't want to. I saw all I ever needed to see from back there. Are you okay?'

He nodded and she touched his big arm.

'We better call somebody,' she said. 'You want me to grab your phone?'

Baron stroked his goatee. His cheeks grew round as he let out a heavy and thoughtful sigh and gazed toward the lights of the caravan.

'You know I can't do that,' he said. 'Not with the rap sheet of this crew. They'd probably haul half of us away when they started asking questions.'

'We can drive on down the road and call it.'

'I don't think so. I put my hands on him and I probably shouldn't have but it's over. And I ain't interested in talking to anybody in a uniform about it. You know somebody will come along soon enough and call it in.'

'I guess so. He's not hurting anymore.'

He tossed the flashlight into the open window of the Suburban and reached out and took the cigarette she was smoking. He sucked on it and looked up and down the highway and then as he walked a small circle of contemplation in front of the Suburban his foot kicked a full envelope that had been hiding in the dark. He flicked the cigarette away and bent down and picked it up and there was no doubt what was inside. Only a matter of how much.

'What is it?' Annette asked when she saw that he was holding something.

'Come here,' he said. She joined him in front of the hood and he opened the envelope. Fluttered the stacks with his thumb. Then they exchanged the unsteady look of two people standing at a crossroads.

'Damn,' she said.

From down the line someone blew the horn and he knew curiosity would soon have others standing there with him.

'Walk it with me one more time,' he said. 'Make sure there's nobody else laying out here.'

He shoved the envelope into his belt line and draped his shirt over it. He and Annette walked around the truck and toward the crop and then again toward the caravan when they made the lap without further discovery.

'You want to do it again?' she asked.

But he said no. Probably shouldn't haven't done it a second time. He scanned the scene once more and was reassured there were no footprints on the dry ground. And then he said we need to get out of here before somebody comes along. I don't think I need to tell you all of this stays between you and me.

6

THE WALLS OF THE JUKEJOINT WERE lined with sheets of tin and random, ageless signs strung by fishing line onto giant steel bolts. Dixie Beer. RC Cola. Sunbeam Bread. Fluorescent lights hung from the beams of an exposed ceiling by coat hangers. A jukebox that had never played a song sat in the corner, covered in layers of grime and dust that cloaked its antique features.

Jack sat up straight. Wiped sweat from the beer can in front of him and ran his wet hand across his face and then he picked up the beer and killed it. An empty shot glass was beside the can and Jack held it and looked for somebody to fill it.

Sitting on a makeshift stage in a folding chair was a black man in overalls. A cigarette dangled from his mouth and he picked an unplugged Fender. With him on the crowded plywood stage were two more folding chairs, a couple of mic stands, a stripped down drum kit consisting of only a kickdrum, snare, two cymbals. No chairs or tables across the concrete floor. Jack watched him in silence for a moment, the quiet bend and hammer of the electric strings like faint echoes in the brokedown barroom. He and the man onstage were the only two there.

The man paused and took the cigarette from his mouth and saw Jack. 'You want something?' he asked.

He reached into his pocket and found the plastic bag. He opened it and took out a pill and dropped it in his mouth. 'Something to chase that with,' he said.

The man moved behind the bar and took a bottle of Old Crow from the wooden shelf on the wall. He filled the shot glass. Reached into the cooler and took out two cans and slid one to Jack and opened one for himself. Jack took the shot. Stared at the empty glass. Tried to think.

'Who brought me in here?' he asked.

'Nobody.'

Jack rubbed at his eyes. Held them closed and searched the dark behind them.

'A woman,' he said. 'Some woman came with me.'

The man shook his head. Shirtless under his overalls. Baggy, wrinkled eyes. Long fingers and big knuckles and dryskinned shoulders. 'Ain't seen no woman.'

'White hair, maybe. Lots of it.'

'Ain't seen no woman. Whitehaired, blackhaired, bluehaired. You stumbled in the door like a crazy man. Nose dripping blood and babbling shit and I propped you up and you had a few shots and fell out dead.'

'Why the hell didn't you call somebody?'

'I ain't got no phone.'

Jack put his head down on the bar. The whitehaired woman and her hand on his arm and her whispers adrift in his mind. He couldn't hold on to her so he let it go and then he asked about his truck.

'Must be down the road,' the man said. He leaned his back against the wall. Arms folded.

Jack laid his head down again. Wanted the booze to come on and work. Wanted the pain pill to come on and work.

'You ain't going to sleep again. We both leaving. Night's gone.'

'I ain't going to sleep.'

'Then pick your head up. I got to go. And you owe me twenty dollars.'

Jack stood from the barstool. There was no money in his front pockets. A fold of bills in his back pocket and a note. He laid twenty dollars on the bar and then he read the note. 12K straight to Big Momma Sweet.

'Shit,' he said.

'What is it?'

'Only all I needed to know,' he said and he laid another ten on the bar. 'Here's a little extra if you'll get me to my truck.'

They came outside and the early dawn gave blue in the east and purple to the west. A long-eared dog sniffed around the gravel parking lot and the man reached into his pocket and tossed a dog biscuit on the ground. The dog picked it up and held it in its mouth and disappeared around the side of the building. The only vehicle in the parking lot was a flatbed work truck and he and Jack got in and they headed along the highway in the direction that Jack guessed he had come from.

'That's it,' Jack said as they approached, pointing off the side of the road. 'Tell me you got a winch that works.'

'I got a winch that works.'

The truck had skidded to a stop just before disturbing the crop rows. The work truck had a winch on front and the man slowed and stopped, his front end facing the overturned bottom of Jack's vehicle, the back end of the truck sticking out onto the highway. The two men got out and Jack stood with his hands on his hips. The man held his hands in the pockets of his overalls. They looked at the truck as if it might tell them what happened.

'You ain't supposed to be driving all messed up,' the man said and he moved to the back end and walked along the trail of sunken earth where the truck had slid on its side.

Jack said just help me get it upright and we can be done. He walked to the winch and lifted the large iron hook and was looking for a release for the cable when he heard the man let out a quick yell.

'What?' Jack called.

'Aw hell no. Hell no,' the man said. He was walking toward the work truck and shaking his head.

'What is it?'

'I got to go.'

'We're not done.'

'I am. Go look over yonder,' he said and he waved toward the crops.

Jack moved around the end of his overturned truck and he saw the body. Legs bent back and dried blood on the dead man's face and mouth. Flies buzzing about his head. Jack dropped to one knee and propped his head onto his balled fist as if thinking or praying or repenting or a little of it all.

The man climbed in the work truck and slammed the door.

'Where you going?'

'Away from here.'

'Help me get it turned upright.'

'I ain't staying here with a dead white boy.'

Jack left the body and hurried over. Put his hands on the hood and said you don't even have to get out. Just let me hook it up and pull it.

The old man cranked the truck and stared at Jack. 'Son of a bitch you got about thirty seconds to get that damn thing hitched and then you pretend like you never seen me,' he said and he pulled a latch under the dashboard. The winch was freed and Jack took the hook and walked over to his truck. He reached up and dropped the hook over the front axle and then made a loop with the cable and then he gave the old man a thumbs up.

There was another click and the winch retracted and the cable pulled straight. The metal groaned as the truck began to tip and then the weight came and it landed flat with a dusty thud.

'Unhook that shit,' the man yelled. Jack eased himself onto the ground and he lay on his back, sliding under the truck and removing the hook and cable. As the cable retracted Jack spotted a folded blue tarp strapped to the truck bed with a bungee cord and he walked over and snatched it just as the man put the truck in reverse and backed onto the highway. The man then shifted into drive and was gone in a clunky instant, tires spinning and hollering something about the dead and the dying and the Lord Jesus Christ.

Jack watched him go. And then he turned and looked at his truck. Dented door. Busted headlight. Spiderweb windshield. Bent tailgate. A dead son of a bitch on the other side. He pulled open the door and climbed in, looking for the money on the floorboard and behind the seat and underneath the seat, expecting his hand to find an envelope. To ease the panic. He found instead brass knuckles and a sock and two empty bottles of Tylenol but no envelope. He slid the brass knuckles into his pocket and then walked two laps around the truck and he walked up and down the side of the road and he crossed the highway and looked on the other side and nothing. He ran over to the burrowed trail where the truck had slid and he got down on his knees, his hands digging and slapping at the rich earth and he began to lose his breath and bite at his lip as there was no treasure to be found. His face twisted in anxiety and pain as he raised his eyes and looked at the body and then bits and pieces of the night came back to him. Leaving the casino. Stopping for gas. And then a stranger somewhere and the body had to be the stranger so he got off his knees and stood over the body and then he noticed an approaching car. He brushed the dirt from his hands. From his pants. Stood at the bent tailgate and believed the body was out of sight on the other side of the truck. But he had to wait to find out. The car came closer. Slowed. Jack nodded and gave a halfwave. Then the driver of the car did the same as the vehicle passed and accelerated.

He returned to the body and fought the pain in his back as he lifted and dropped it on the edge of the tarp. He rolled the body in the tarp and then he scooped his arms under and tossed it in the truck bed and then climbed in with it. He worked the end of the tarp down until he saw the top of the head and then he worked it lower and he stared at Skelly's face. Right cheekbone crushed. A crooked jaw. The sight of the face didn't help at all. Jack closed his eyes and searched the black spot in his mind. His face in a grimace of frustration and pressing his fingers against his forehead as if trying to force his thoughts into giving him answers. He heard the jingles and bells of the slot machines and he heard old men laughing but he could see no faces and find no names.

He opened his eyes. Grabbed the back of the neck to hold the body still while he worked the tarp over the head and that's when he felt the brand. He shoved the body on its side and there was the rubbery flesh of the dollar sign. On the back of the neck. The mark of Big Momma Sweet to scar those who owed and to remind them of who they owed it to.

Jack sat down. Touched the tender spot on his forehead. And then he lay down in the truck bed next to the corpse. They are everywhere, he thought. She has them everywhere. And whoever this is knows what happened to the money but he can't tell me. All that matters is it's gone. It won't mean nothing to her for you to blame a dead man, especially one of her own.

And she'll brand you. Right before she kills you. Just for fun. He stared up at the awakening sky. At the soft brushes of clouds moving slowly in the first light and then he draped his arm across his eyes and he imagined his own burning flesh as they held him down and made him take it.

7

SHE BELIEVED SHE COULD HAVE ANYTHING she wanted. But she didn't know what she wanted so she had lived her young adult life guided by her own church of coincidence and she faithfully followed its direction without the necessity of reason or justification, like a fallen leaf trusting its flight to the shifts of a mighty wind.

She traced the beginnings of her doctrine to the simple butterfly tattoo she had gotten on the inside of her wrist on her nineteenth birthday. Black antennas curved like candy canes and the wings colored in crimson and yellow. A butterfly because she had begun to feel her own transformation. Leaving the small apartment she and her mother shared, the bitterness that lived on the edge of each word her mother spoke having become like some stone necklace that held her closer to the ground. Allowing her raven hair to grow from the short cut she had worn through childhood and her teenage years, the black falling down her neck and touching her shoulders and she began to keep it highlighted with streaks of purple or pink or blue. Becoming more aware of her own body. Her legs long and her thighs and calves firm. The curve in the arch of her back when she noticed her own shadow. The soft nape of her neck and her breasts hard and round and the attention the eyes gave her when she walked into anywhere. She worked at a pet store during the day and she waited tables at night and scraped together enough to have her own two-room apartment on the south side of Memphis. Milk crates and empty boxes for furniture. A sleeping bag for a bed. But it was hers. And the only voice she had to listen to was her own.

All of her extra money went to the tattoos. She added more butterflies, a string reaching from her wrist and up her forearm in the pattern of a lazy S and she could never decide if it looked like they were coming or going. Then she moved in with a tattoo shop owner who was a sharp and talented artist and the more he believed that she loved him the more free ink he gave. A litter of stars across the top of each hand. A crown of thorns circling her elbow. Up and down her calves and around her knees wrapped serpents and vines and then she chose clouds and crosses and birds on her thighs as if to offer escape from the venom and thorns twisting below. She loved his work but did not love him as much so when he walked in the door on a spring afternoon and proudly displayed her name tattooed down the side of his neck, she panicked. The suggestion of permanence beyond what she had either considered or desired. For weeks she avoided the question of when she might return the same artful gesture and she instead added a sleek hot rod across the small of her back. A woman driving with a thick mane of black and purple hair flapping in the wind. Then she added the wings to her shoulder blades and to the tops of her feet, believing the symbols of flight and movement may give him the notion that she wasn't going to be there much longer. But it didn't and he kept asking. Where will you put my name? She could not make herself tell him I can't do it. So instead she left a note on the table that said what she hoped was a soft goodbye.

She left but she didn't have a plan. Only knew she wasn't going to wait tables any longer. Wasn't going back to a sleeping bag on the floor. Her two-door Toyota crammed full of clothes and a bedspread and pillow and a couple of boxes and she drove around Memphis all day with her windows down, looking and listening for an answer. Past the old neighborhoods surrounding Rhodes College and the hip streets lining the university.

Graceland and the tour buses. The corporate stretches of hotels and restaurants and big stores that joined Memphis and Germantown. And in her crossing the city she noticed the strip club billboards. Noticed the clean white skin of the women who posed with their hands on their hips and their chests stuck out and she thought there was no way they didn't just bore the hell out of the men who paid to sit and watch. What they need is an attraction, she thought. Something to admire. Something to examine. Something that will make their eyes look in places they aren't accustomed to looking. What they need is me.

She bought a quart of beer and drove to the river. Parked and sat on the hood of the car and watched the muddy water and the strip of clouds that hung in the west in the late day sun. Maybe it made sense, she thought. Maybe it didn't. A drop of sweat dripped from the bottle and landed on her leg and ran down the inside of her thigh. A steamboat horn echoed across the river and she lifted her eyes and across the horizon the clouds were flushed in pink and lavender and the sky grabbed her and said you are like me. You are your own beautiful thing. She set the quart bottle on the ground and then she dug a bikini top out of the backseat. Slipped off her shirt and bra and tied on the top. Rolled her shorts higher and pushed them down some on her hips. She wanted to show all the ink-covered curves when she walked in and said I'm available. Your masterpiece is here.

She left the river and the next billboard she saw was for the

Stallion. On the east side of Memphis and out by the airport. Miles and miles of giving up. Empty strip malls with plywood covering the windows and check cashing stores and liquor stores. Rental furniture and pawnshops and discount tobacco and used cars. Every now and then a tamale stand. Stragglers pushing shopping carts filled with aluminum cans and hubcaps. Standing tall among the rabble was the pink sign with the horse reared on its hind legs and THE STALLION written beneath in broad black letters. The marquee below the pink sign advertised half price drinks and then at the bottom of the marquee it read DANCERS WANTED.

Annette pulled into the parking lot and parked between a Corvette and a BMW. Both vehicles slick clean and with tinted windows. Standing on each side of the front door were short and stout men wearing tight pink shirts that gripped their chests and biceps. Annette got out and walked across the parking lot as college boys piled out of a pickup and one whistled at her and another shouted I thought the show was inside. When she climbed the steps to the front door the men in pink held open the doors for her and she strutted past with a sultry smile, certain of the sexual aura of her tattooed glory.

She liked the money and the attention. Her own image on the billboard. Those who came specifically to see her. The regulars who sat in the same seats on the same nights of the week and who gave her fives and tens and twenties and on the nights when the alcohol told them they had a chance they gave hundreds. The apartment with furniture and the clothes and the power she held as she moved and provided them with the unique and artful display of the flesh.

What she did not like was living her life in the dark. The dark of the showroom and the dark of night when she arrived and when she left. The dark faces that told her what they thought she wanted to hear with dark voices and dark hands sliding closer to her dark body. Never eating a breakfast because she slept through the days and woke in the late afternoon to find that things had happened in the world while she danced or dreamed. The weather had shifted or a movie she wanted to see had come and gone from the theater or there had been an alert for a missing child and the child had been found. The world continued to spin while they gawked at her from cushioned chairs.

Two years walked past and toward the end of her Stallion days she would stand on the balcony of her apartment as the day disappeared and look across the pool of the apartment complex. The last orange light against the vinyl siding of the apartment buildings reminding her of the day at the river when she chose this life. The pool water flat and still in the twilight and then she would try and leave her melancholy there with the terracotta pot filled with her cigarette butts and bottle caps. Go into the bedroom and take off her clothes and stare at herself in the mirror on the bathroom door. Then she would shower and eat something and by then it was night.

She did not know her last night at the Stallion was going to be her last night when she arrived. She did not know it as she walked into the dressing room and talked to the other girls. Did not know it as she put on her makeup and sprayed glitter in her hair and rubbed lotion all over her body. Did not know it as she pulled on her costume with gold wings and a gold sequin mask and then sat smoking a cigarette and waiting on her turn and did not know it when she stepped behind the curtain and listened to her name being announced and then heard the applause and the music. Did not know it as the smoke machine and laser lights created her entrance and she stepped high onto the stage and down the runway and made her first slow turn to show them every side of what they were about to get.

She knew it when she reached for the pole and the spotlight caught the original butterfly on her wrist. Surrounded now by so many more tattoos she had forgotten it but in that brief flash she missed the daylight and she missed the woman who had gritted her teeth as the needle gun buzzed and she bled and watched the butterfly become a part of her as she reveled in the act of transformation. She kept her eyes on the butterfly and the trail of others that followed as she swung around the pole but she decided she wasn't going to give it to them anymore.

She let go of the pole. Walked to the edge of the stage. She took off the mask and tossed it into the crowd. Reached behind her neck and unclipped the clasp that held the wings and they dropped from her arms and to the floor. She stood and stared out at the shadowy figures and the smoke that hung above their heads and the music played and when she didn't move a voice called out for her to get on with it.

She turned her head to the voice and said what are you looking at. Then she moved her eyes from one side of the stage to the other and asked them all the same question. Louder each time. What are you looking at?

Some yelled back and some booed. The DJ cut the music.

She held out her arms and asked again and this time they all could hear. Those in the seats next to the stage and those in the seats in the rear and those sitting at the bar and the waitresses and bartenders and the girl taking the cover charge and the thick men in the tense pink shirts.

'What the hell are you looking at?' she yelled.

She dropped her arms and as the frustrated crowd groaned and insulted she stripped out of her costume and stepped out of the heels. She left it all right there and she walked naked across the stage. Through the curtain. Into the dressing room. She pulled on a robe and grabbed her keys and purse and was out the back door.

8

THE OUTLAW CARNIVAL WAS JUST THAT. The workers mostly ex-cons or parole jumpers or hiding from alimony but that didn't bother Baron because he had been into a little of it all himself in his sixty years. He hired them and let them drive his trucks and trailers. Let them run the carnival games and rides and he paid them every Friday and he had only two rules. Be where you're supposed to be when I tell you to be there and if you get busted don't call me. He hired them but he didn't trust them and he damn sure wasn't going to walk around with twelve thousand dollars cash.

Baron had led the trail of vehicles to the outskirts of Clarksdale after leaving the wrecked truck and the body and the caravan pulled into a mobile home park an hour before dawn. A shirtless man wearing jeans and suspenders came out of a trailer at the park entrance. He announced himself as the manager and asked what the hell they thought they were doing. Baron held out a hundred dollar bill and said we're looking for a place to hunker down for a day and get some rest and the man pulled at his suspenders. Took the money. Said go all the way to the end of the road where won't nobody see you and complain. You wouldn't believe the shit I have to hear about. Damn dog barks and they come running.

The caravan moved through the mobile home park with its usual array of rattles and chugs and at the far end came upon several empty lots next to one another. Baron parked the Suburban and directed traffic and by the time the sun came up the caravan was parked in neat rows and sleeping.

But he did not sleep. Not with what he had seen and what he had done. Not with the envelope hidden beneath the mattress he slept on in the rear of the Suburban and as he sat in a lawn chair and smoked cigarette after cigarette he wondered about the money and its origins. The envelope had a casino logo but he had seen the pills and whiskey bottles. He had seen the bulging eyes and sunken jaw of the dead man. And he knew he was in the middle of nowhere in Mississippi where nobody carried that kind of cash unless there was a damn good reason and he tried to think of the best way to both get rid of it and keep it.

The bluegray of dawn. A solitary cloud hanging next to the fading moon. Flocks of blackbirds like flapping dots in the morning sky and the sound of doors opening and closing around the trailer park as the early ones left for work. Baron stood from the lawn chair and tossed away a cigarette. Stretched his big arms and bent his back and then he saw Annette climb out of her boxlike camper and he was relieved by her appearance.

He had first thought of her the way most men thought of her. He imagined doing things to her and what she might do to him but that feeling drifted away as she soon became a much needed relief from the macho men on the payroll. As close to a friend as he thought he could have. She had simply walked up to the carnival one day. Rides spinning and popcorn popping and across the lot came this artful thing and he not only noticed her but noticed the way that the heads turned when she walked by wearing a short skirt and tanktop. Her arms and legs covered in designs of blacks and reds and blues and she owned the body to exhibit. The children had looked in wonder. The mothers in jealousy or loathing. The men with openmouthed curiosity. She had stopped and asked for the bossman at the ticket booth and by the time she had crossed the carnival grounds and introduced herself he was already trying to think of a way to use her ability to lure.

Now she sat in the empty lawn chair next to him. Pulled a rubber band from her wrist and put her hair in a ponytail.

'You should be sleeping,' he said.

'So should you.'

'Well. I can't.'

'Me neither. Where is it?'

'In there,' he said and he nodded at the vehicle. And then he lowered his voice and said I counted it. Twelve thousand. I can't figure out what to do with it.

'Divide it up.'

He shook his head. 'There is no such thing as a democracy when it comes to money. Besides, then everybody will know where it come from. And I don't need that headache. These boys didn't gain employment by singing in the choir.'

'Then give me half and you take half. You know I won't say nothing.'

'There's something in it for you. But not half.'

'Why not half?'

'Because I'm the one that will answer one day for what happened back there.'

'You think you did something wrong?'

'I don't know. What do you think?'

'I think it'll take more than what's in that envelope to cover whatever sins you believe you might have.'

He stroked his goatee. Scratched at his cheek.

Annette crossed her legs and yawned. 'Why don't you do what any good American would do and put it in the bank?' she asked.

'I don't have an account nowhere. Then the IRS would know where to find me. It's taken a lifetime of ducking and dodging to stay hid from them.'

'Burn it then.'

'What?'

'You got to do something,' she said. 'Give it away. It's not the lottery jackpot but it's the kind of money that could change somebody's life.'

Across the lot the carnival workers appeared at random, coming out of their trailers and crawling out of their truck cabs like the weary survivors of a storm.

'I think I'll just let you have it,' he said.

'Whatever.'

'Really. You take it. Do something with it. Whatever you want except running off.'

'I don't want to mess with it,' she said and she shifted in the chair. Shook her head.

'How come?'

'Not sure. Feels like when I got my palm read one time. I knew it was all bullshit but I couldn't help but feel uneasy about what I'd heard.' She leaned forward and slipped a cigarette out of the pack on the ground. 'Besides. Whatever I do with it you won't like.'

'I told you I don't care.'

'That's not like you, Baron. You're making me nervous. What is it?'

'Nothing.'

'Does it bother you that bad? What you did?'

'No. Not so much. All I did was send him where he was already going.'

'Then what is it?'

He lifted a lighter and lit her cigarette.

'I guess I'm like you. Uneasy about it. This money can't lead nowhere but somewhere really bad or somewhere really good. Sounds like that crazy church idea you're always talking about. And I ain't really in the mood for extremities.'

'You believe in my church now?'

'I didn't say I believe in it. I said it sounds like it. The church of cooperation. That it?'

'Coincidence,' she said. 'The church of coincidence. You know what it is. It brought me to you.'

'I guess. And now something brought this money to us. That how it goes?'

He lit another cigarette. He smoked and then said I know you'll handle the money better than me. If you want it. But I don't. I wish I would've left it laying there in the dirt. Just whatever you do don't run off.

'You said that already.'

'And I meant it both times. I've heard enough about your story to know it doesn't take much for your winds to change.'

'There's nothing wrong with my winds.'

'Maybe we'll call it a donation to your church. That's tax deductible.'

'Except you don't pay taxes.'

'Yep. And never will.'

He held the cigarette between his lips and pushed himself up from the chair with the armrests. Then he said let's take a ride. That's the best way for me to give the envelope to you. Away from here and all these hounddogs.

Ricky Joe lay on a mattress in the back of the El Camino. The windows of the camper shell dirty and damp on the outside from the morning dew but when he heard their voices he lifted his head and saw them clearly enough.

He shifted to his side, unlatched the window and it opened a few inches. In a pile of clothes he dug for cigarettes and kept one eye on Baron and Annette. They spoke in what he could only hear as mumbles and then they got in the Suburban together. Rolled down the windows. Her long and lanky arm hanging out as they drove away.

No cigarettes but he found a can of root beer. He raised the hatch of the shell and he climbed out and sat on the hood of the El Camino shirtless and barefoot. He opened the warm root beer. The other carnival workers milled around with cigarettes or instant coffee. They opened trunks or trailer cabinets and took out small gas grills and skillets. Opened coolers and found butter and bread or eggs or packets of ham.

He had snuck out of the El Camino during the night while the caravan was pulled to the side of the road. He had heard Baron tell them all to stay put but then he had seen Annette walking with him and he slid across the bench seat and slipped out, moving into the kneehigh cotton and pretending to piss as a voice from the vehicle behind the El Camino told him to get his ass in the car and do what Baron said. He was out of the caravan headlights so he knelt in the field as he watched them searching the scene. Watched when they paused and Baron knelt to pick something up. Watched them talk about it and then watched as they returned to their vehicles. And he had seen the body. Or what he thought was a body. The silhouette of some figure that could have only been the dead. He hurried out of the crops and into the El Camino as the caravan moved again.

The carnival had been his traveling home for only a few weeks. Right out of doing ninety days in the Bolivar County lockup for simple assault. His hand flat against the ass of a woman in the supermarket checkout line and her husband smacking a can of creamed corn into his nose and then the two men taking out the candy bar and battery racks before the wheezing security guard could get there from his comfy chair in the break room. The county lockup familiar to him but this time when he got out he came upon the carnival on the side of an empty furniture warehouse. He carried a tallboy in a paperbag as he strode about and looked for something worth stealing and then there was a loud metal grind and a flush of smoke when the engine for the Tilt-A-Whirl seized up. He was entertained by the screaming children stuck in midride and entertained watching them rescued one by one and more entertained watching the huddle of men who stood around the engine, unable to figure out what to do.

'I can fix it,' he finally said.

'Who are you?' asked a big man with a braided ponytail.

'It really don't matter. Does it?'

Baron had studied him. Redeyed and squirrely but seemingly certain of his ability. 'Fix it then,' he said.

Ricky Joe had grown up in a mob of brothers and sisters. Uncles and aunts and cousins. All living in three mobile homes on the edge of a junkyard owned by his grandfather. Some cars in the junkyard were crushed. Others they tried to repair and make their own and he grew up trying to help resuscitate vehicles that were graveyard bound. So the engine of the Tilt-A-Whirl appeared to him as no bigger a problem than two plus two. He knelt next to the engine and they gave him room and in thirty minutes the Tilt-A-Whirl was spinning again and Baron offered him a job. He took it.

But he wasn't interested in this job anymore. He was interested in what he had seen the night before. Two people at the scene of an accident interested in something more than the accident itself. He sipped the root beer and scratched at his belly. Baron is not the play, he thought. You won't get nothing from him except turned out of the carnival. It's her. She's the one.

9

JACK CLIMBED OUT OF THE TRUCK bed. The top of the sun over the edge of the horizon as he stared at the truck and said no I don't expect you to crank but I wish you would before I have to explain what's in this blue tarp to somebody.

He crawled under and realized the dripping was from a cracked radiator and if it wasn't already all leaked out it would be soon. He slid out from under and got in. The keys still in the ignition. He turned the key and the engine chugged but then caught. It coughed and smoke came from the engine and from the tailpipe and he didn't wait to see how long it would last. He shifted into drive and the truck gagged and almost died but then it jerked forward and then smoothed and in a few miles he came to Clarksdale.

He drove through the tired downtown with the grand old buildings that had suffered decades of apathy. Rainstreaked facades and faded FOR SALE signs in windows and barrelsized flowerpots with white and purple petunias running over the sides as if serving as a small reminder of the color of possibility. And then the bricked streets of downtown turned into the patched roads that passed the government housing and trailer parks that finally gave way to the green and spacious. He turned left on Highway 1 and drove past a gas station. A policeman leaned on the hood of his patrol car looking at the newspaper and when the smoking truck with the busted windshield passed by he looked up. Jack slumped in the seat a little. Raised his hand and waved and the cop nodded.

Along the highway he began to look for the house off the road in the same way that he had always looked for it on the school bus in the afternoon. His time with Maryann stretching on and his clothes in the same room and the rhythm of life unfamiliar to him so he remained distrustful and looked for the house out of the window as if it wasn't going to be there. As if she wasn't going to be there. That the bus would take him somewhere different and drop him off and the driver would tell him good luck as he climbed off and tried to figure out what to do next.

But it was always there.

He turned into the gravel driveway and rolled along, the house back from the road and flanked by oak trees. The grass and summer weeds high and several shingles missing from the roof. The white more like gray and pieces of frame hanging here and there. A crow sitting atop a post that served as one end of a clothesline. He parked and rubbed at his chin. Took his notebook and got out, walking around antbeds and fallen limbs and stepping over the petite petals of wildflowers. A window screen loose and folded back. He stepped onto the front porch and noticed the droppings of some kind of animal. On the front door a copy of the foreclosure notice had been posted.

The first night he had spent at Maryann's house he slept late and when he opened his eyes he had to think. Remember where he was. Remember who he was with. Thin curtains allowed the sunshine into the highceiling room and he put his feet on the floor and looked around. A painting of a horse and woman in a field on one wall and black and white photographs of some cityscape were arranged in a rectangle on another. A rug much too small for the space of the hardwood floor lay between the bed and the door and three bulky and warped candles sat on a brass tray on the marble top of a corner table.

He had come down the stairs and the wall was lined with more photographs. Some of the photos black and white and some so old they were shades of gray and sepia and others in color but the colors washed with time. Photos of children sitting on a porch and brides and grooms beneath the same arched trellis and an old man leaning against a tree and a man and woman posing with their arms propped on the hood of a tractor. An endless trail of faces as Jack moved down the stairs and he had stopped in the middle of the staircase and paid close attention to a man with a mustache. His arms folded and a cigarette in his hand. A gray tweed coat. Jack pretended to take the cigarette from his hand and he took an imaginary puff and tossed it over the banister and then he descended and looked for the woman who had showed him the bedroom the day before.

He had gone into the kitchen and through the open door he saw her in the backyard. She was opening bags of mulch and spreading it across a freshly dug flower bed that circled the thin trunk of a young Japanese maple. She wore jeans too big rolled to her knees and a sweatshirt with the sleeves cut off. Her hair in waves and stuck to her sweaty forehead. He tried to think of her name and when she saw him she called out. Said come on. I want to show you something.

They walked across the yard. She had asked what he liked to eat for breakfast and he said whatever you got. She then took him into a spacious one-room building on the edge of the backyard that bumped right up against the crop rows. Shutter windows that stayed swung open in the heat of early summer and two ceiling fans circulating overhead. A wide plank floor and the back wall lined with shelves from floor to ceiling and resting on the shelves were ceramic plates and bowls of all sizes. Planting pots and serving platters and coffee mugs. All in different stages as some were unfinished pieces, dry and chalky and the color of mud. Others of the same color but shiny with a coat of varnish and still other shelves held the finished productions. Vases and pots and bowls that had been painted and coated and dotted with tiny price stickers.

Around the room had been a couple of stools and square wooden tables. Dropcloths in a folded stack in the corner. Tubes of paint and paintbrushes sat in a wide plastic tray on one of the tables and a double sink splattered in color was beneath an open window. Aprons hung on hooks on the wall. A handcrafted potter's wheel sat in the middle of the room, the dust and trails of a hundred years of work seeped into the rustcolored grain of its tabletop and bench legs.

'What do you think?' she had asked as they stood in the doorway. 'This is the potter's barn. At least that's what my mom and grandma called it.' The boy looked around curiously and then he stepped inside and walked over and ran his finger across the flat circular slab of the wheel.

'That's called a potter's wheel,' she said. 'But it's old. They make electric ones now but my grandma taught me how to use this one when I was about your age and it's the only one I'll have.'

'What does it do?' he asked.

She had waved her hand toward the shelves and said it makes all of this.

'How?' he said.

She told him about how she had learned watching her grandmother and she explained the process and how long a piece needed to sit and dry and what kept your work from splitting and cracking and why it was important to put your initials on the bottom of each piece so that when you sold it that part of you would always be there. And sometimes the piece would be passed on from one family to the next. And a little of you would live wherever that bowl or vase lived. He had asked questions about the wheel and about mixing paints and he had asked how she decided how much a piece cost and where she sold them and she answered all his questions and was happy that he had them.

'Why?' he finally asked.

'Why what?'

'Why do you do it?'

'I'm not a farmer and don't really know anything about all that land out there except who I lease it to,' she said. 'I like to use my hands. Start with nothing and end up with something.'

He had walked over to the wall and taken an apron from the hook and slid it over his head. The end of the apron touched the floor and she asked if he wanted to try.

He looked at the wheel and then looked at the work on the shelves. 'No,' he said. 'I'll just mess it up.'

'There is no messing it up,' she said. 'Just try.'

'Not right now,' he had said again and he removed the apron and returned it to the hook. 'Maybe I could watch you do it?'

'All right.'

'But can we eat something first?'

They had walked out of the potter's barn and as they moved up the steps of the porch and toward the kitchen door he said I need to ask you one more thing. What is your name?

Now he snatched the foreclosure notice from the front door and paced and the boards creaked beneath his feet as he chastised this other self. This other Jack who did things he could not remember and somehow thought he could get away with it. This other Jack who walked and talked and signed papers and lied and cheated and lost and then did not have to face the consequences as he left it all for him to clean up. The one who stood at the end of his mistakes where all the Jacks collided.

He stopped and sat down on the steps. Opened the notebook and read. He needed thirty thousand dollars to keep the house from going to sale to the public, a sheriff standing on the front steps of the courthouse and auctioning the property to buyers who would get it for a fraction of its value. The years and history and generations of Maryann's family who had lived there and wedded there and died there disappearing with a raise of the hand to the highest bidder. He made another checkmark on the foreclosure notice. From eight days down to seven days. But it might as well have been seven minutes. He searched the pages of the notebook for a note or a name, some clue to who might let him borrow enough to keep Big Momma at a distance and delay the foreclosure but he knew there was no such answer.

Two days after he turned forty he was sidekicked in the head by a much younger and quicker man and he was out before he hit the smooth clay of the fighting pit. He flopped unconscious and he took two more hard fists to the temple before it was called. He woke in a hospital room and he didn't know his own name or where he was or how he got there and they gave him enough painkillers to dull a horse but the pain burned through in his head and neck in aggressive and arrogant flames. For days he lay in the hospital room in the great blank spaces of his mind with the whole world a stranger and he stared out of the window with a blissful unawareness of regret or loss. He left the hospital with a ringing in his head that hadn't been there before and a prescription for painkillers that carried a strength his body craved. Those tiny pills that released him for a little while. Allowed him to sleep. To sit up straight. Beginning to take an extra one in the mornings when it was difficult to get out of bed or when the sun was too bright against his eyes and the prescriptions disappeared more quickly. Going from one doctor to the next and trying to get refills and when that no longer worked he turned to the other fighters. Men with their own addictions and their own dealers. Paying cash in locker rooms or in parking lots at the venues, getting connected with dealers he trusted to eventually taking whatever he could get from whoever he could get it from. The headaches had been steady for ten years but now he carried something sharper, more violent, inside his brain, a pain unlike he had known and a headache that would seize him at any instant. Take him to his knees. A pain that searched for a weakness in the medication he kept pumping into his body and when there was a pause, when he tried to lay off and let himself be, this new headache gripped and said who do you think you are? You can't hold back. You better take it all the time whether you need it or not or I will cripple you.

Along the highway in front of the house a log truck bellowed as it shifted gears. The crow flew from the clothesline post and landed in the tall grass of the front yard, pecked around and then flew away with a bug in its beak. Jack then stood and walked to the back door.

He stepped inside the kitchen. The air was stagnant and he left the door open and raised the window above the sink. On the small table where he learned to drink coffee and eat things grown in the garden he set down the notebook and emptied his pockets.

Four red and three blue pills and a fold of cash. Some change and a cigarette lighter and the brass knuckles.

He walked through the house. Blades of sunlight slicing between spaces in curtains and blinds and making golden stripes across the hardwood. A heavy air and tiny dust diamonds moving across the light and Jack stepping slowly from room to room as if anticipating an ambush. His eyes careful around each corner and through each doorway and some strange fear rising in him as he moved throughout the sleeping house. No furniture. He had years ago loaded the armoires and handcrafted tables and mahogany headboards and everything else that had any value onto a U-Haul truck and then he drove out on the thin dirt road between the acreage, to a shack Maryann's father had long ago strengthened with new framing and converted into a storage shed. He unloaded and put a combination lock on the door but he didn't write down the numbers of the combination, trying to keep the furniture from ending up on a pawnshop floor.

Only shadows across empty rooms, chandeliers dulled by a thick film of dust and cobwebs spun in the corners of the ceilings and window frames. The shift of light and shadow and he felt the sensation of moving out of one world and into another. The house a museum of life passed by.

He climbed the stairs and ran his finger across the picture frames to wipe the dust away and when he got to the top he looked down over the banister. Waited as if maybe the ghosts he always imagined to be in here would slide out from behind their supernatural cover and welcome him. But there was only the sound of his own labored breathing from climbing the stairs and he moved into the upstairs hallway and went into what had been his bedroom.

He crossed the room and stood at the foot of his bed. The only piece of furniture he did not have carted away. He set his gnarly knuckles on the top of the metal footboard and like he had done many times before, after listening to Maryann talk about mothers and great grandfathers and grandmothers and great aunts, he imagined the lives that had been lived in this house. The bare feet of old people and children that had crossed this floor in the first warm days of spring and the eyes that had closed in this bed and the dreams that came to those of past generations but still dreams of the same things. Of love and belonging and of a hand to hold and of flying and being embraced in just the right way. And dreams overrun by the eternal wolves of fear and loss until the body jerked and the eyes opened. In times when he could not sleep as a boy he would imagine the spirits of all those other lives coming and lying with him and escorting him into a peaceful sleep.

He looked up from the bed. I was good, he thought.

He had been young and fierce and every now and then someone knew enough French to call him The Butcher. He stared at the wall and he remembered this younger man and then he remembered the small town seized by an ice storm that snapped tree limbs and took down electrical lines and closed roads. The voices on the radio telling everyone to stay at home and do not drive. Build a fire if you have a fireplace. Take all precaution and help one another. Jack trapped in a motel room without any heat or electricity and the fights canceled and nothing to do. No telephone and no television and he did push-ups and sit-ups to keep warm. His twenty-fifth birthday less than a month away and his reputation growing and his confidence growing and believing he was always worth a ticket. He was in the main event on some nights and on other nights those who had seen him fight told him he should have been. A steady circuit of events across the southeast, as far over as Greensboro and as high up as Lexington and sometimes he went over into Texas and Oklahoma and the venues were clean and sold concessions and had seats.

To shake the chill he had worked up a small sweat doing push-ups and jumping jacks. Boxing himself in the mirror. And then took off his shirt and admired his muscular body before the cold covered him again. He put on a dry shirt and then he went outside to see.

There was beauty in the ice that covered everything. Like nothing he had ever seen. Crystallized trees and silver icicles and the way that time seemed to hold still under the grip of the ice and cold and he could not help but wander and admire. The blanket from the motel room bed wrapping him threefold and his mouth and lips gone dry in an instant. Small clouds of breath from his mouth and nose and he sneaked a hand out from the blanket and touched the tips of straight and silver pine needles. He broke icicles from the ledge of the low roof and bit off the ends. He walked around the front of the motel, the dead grass like breaking glass beneath his feet and he moved onto the slick sidewalk. He followed it with skating steps until he came to a street lined with leafless dogwoods and he gazed at their seized skeletons and imagined them to be ageless, caged warriors waiting to be freed by the sun. With wide eyes he marveled at the frigid and brilliant brush of Mother Nature. He turned back toward the motel and as he turned his head to catch a squirrel sliding down the base of a tree his feet went out from under him. His hands wrapped inside the blanket and nothing to break his fall and his head whiplashed on the icy concrete. A moment of black and then a dizzying gray sky and he lay still for a minute.

He rolled to his side and got his hands free and pressed them against the ice. Raised to his hands and knees. A strike of pain through the back of his head and he crawled along the sidewalk, his knees sliding wide and gathering them back again. He came to a mailbox post and used it to pull himself to his feet. He held on. Let his eyes catch up. And then he very carefully made it to the room and except for going to the vending machine or knocking on the manager's door and asking for aspirin he did not leave again until two days later when the temperature rose and the ice melted away. He did not know he had a concussion, only knew he felt different and when he fought a night later in another town he was slow to react. Feeling as if he was lost in a dream where his arms and hands would not do what he wanted them to do but instead were being controlled by some sleeping part of his mind that would not wake up. He was slow and he paid for it and after the fight the headache that would not go away in the frozen days in the motel room became the headache that brought double vision and neck pain and it became the headache that would forever need something stronger.

Now in the sweltering house his hands turned cold at the memory and he removed them from the footboard. Blew on them though there was sweat across his lip and down the sides of his face. He wanted to lie down in the bed where he slept as a boy and spread his arms and welcome those other lives. Ask them to come and deliver that peace and if it was possible to ask the gods and monsters that lurked on the other side to take him all the way back and give him a chance to begin again.

He went down the stairs and opened the notebook, flipping through the pages until he came to the drawing. A rectangle with four stubby legs and underneath the image were the words *In her closet.* And beneath that *No.*

He closed the notebook and set it on the table and he walked to the end of the hallway. He went inside her bedroom and to the closet. He scanned the shelves and then he knelt and he found the jewelry box on the floor, shoved into the corner. He dragged it out of the shadow. A white marble top and brass claw feet and inscribed on the inside of the box lid were several words written in Italian. He sat down on the floor. The jewelry box in his lap. He opened it and touched his fingers to the inscription and tried to remember what it meant. Inside the box a stack of notes lay on top of the jewelry, all of the notes written in his own hand. And they all said the same thing.

Leave this alone.

He lifted them out and counted. There were five notes and they were dated and covered the span of three years, the first written about the time he stopped staying at the house when he was in Clarksdale because he no longer trusted himself. And he wondered how many more times he had opened the box and seen the notes and walked away. Followed his own orders. He shifted through the notes and the first one had been written in cursive. The second used an exclamation point. The last three he had written in all capital letters. He then set the notes on top of the jewelry and set the box on the floor.

Gone were the two hundred acres that should have never belonged to him in the first place, a foster mother signing over the family home and land to the man she had taken in as a roughedged twelve-year-old. Dementia closing in and nothing to do but move into a home and sign it all over to Jack though the lawyer begged her not to. She held the pen close to the document and said I'm sixty years old and can decide for myself and the lawyer rubbed at his temples while the ink hit the page. A long curl falling from a bobby pin and draping the side of her wrinkled blue eye.

He came back and forth to see Maryann. To sit with her and reintroduce himself. To show her photographs of them together and they would walk in the garden of the yard of the nursing home. Lantanas tall and yellow and butterflies touched their tiny petals and she told him stories he had already heard but he listened and sometimes held her hand if she let him. And then he would stay a few days in the house. Reminded of the simple things she had tried to teach him. Reminded of sunsets and starlit skies and the solace of space. Sit on the upstairs porch in a lawn chair with a pack of cigarettes and a pint of bourbon and feel the silence and feel the pangs of a body breaking down and he would swallow a dozen Tylenol to fight the headaches that were as much a part of him now as skin and bone. Trying to keep off the little red pills when he was there because he imagined her looking over his shoulder. Asking what he was doing. He would sit alone and imagine himself as a boy running across the backyard with his shirt off and swatting fat bumblebees with a tennis racket. Imagine her rocking slowly as she read in the aluminum glider in the afternoon shade of the house. Imagine the miracle it had taken for him to have been delivered to her.

He was only going to do it once. Borrow money against the land and pay everything he owed for the gambling debts and fixes he had blown when he changed his mind in the middle of the fight. As he got older and as he ached more he had begun to work a fix now and then. When he knew the opponent couldn't hurt him until he was ready to be hurt or if the payday for fixing was greater than the payday for winning. But there was one thing he would not take and that was being called old man. He could survive their young muscles and quick hands and cheap shots and drunks standing against the cage calling him names when he didn't seem to be fighting back but only hanging out until it was time to let his hands drop. Take the right punch and then go down and stay down and then get up and collect. He could take all of that. But he could not take it when the opponent said stay down, old man. Or get up and take some more, old man. Or give it up, old man, the young fighters would whisper when they were clutched together. And that was when the transformation began. No matter the fix. No matter the money at stake. No matter how bad he was bleeding or hurt, if his opponent called him an old man it became a different fight.

And the money did not flow in the right direction. And the debts he owed for not doing what he said he was going to do spread from state to state.

Only one time, he had promised himself. And she will never have to know I borrowed the money and I'll come home and get clean. And then figure out what to do. Maybe stay here and get a job doing God knows what but I'll pay it back and she will never know. Just once. He had gone to the bank and got what he needed plus a little more and hit the road. He had driven to Mobile and paid up. Driven to Valdosta and paid up. Driven to Huntsville and tried to pay up but there was an open spot on the card. An easy fight for you, they said. You could walk out of here with your pockets full.

He had eight thousand dollars remaining and he put it all down on himself and then tried to temper a headache with pills and moonshine in the parking lot before the fight. Then was faceplanted on the plywood floor of the ring not sixty seconds after the fight began. And he had been delivered right back into the longfingered grasp of debt.

He looked again at the notes from the jewelry box and they all screamed back in a chorus of his own voice – leave this alone.

He slammed the jewelry box back into the closet and then walked into the kitchen. Took the pill bag from the table and emptied the pills into the sink and then he ran the water and washed them down the drain. Knowing what kind of headache was coming but sick of it all. Sick of the dope and how bad he needed it and sick of the booze and the nausea. Sick of the mounting debts and running from one place to another trying to get even and sick of the sight of himself in the mirror and the thoughts of disloyalty that stuck in his mind whenever he thought about Maryann. He washed his hands and washed his face. Felt the weight upon him from all sides and he had made every excuse for himself since Maryann had gone into the home but that shit was over.

He stuck the money and the lighter and brass knuckles into his pockets and he walked outside. He cranked the truck and drove into the backyard and to the garden hose that fed from the well and he filled the leaking radiator with water. A piece of rope lay next to the potter's barn and he used it to tie up the ends of the tarp and he lifted the body out of the truck bed and hid it behind the potter's barn. He had to get rid of it. He had to face the music with Big Momma Sweet. But that would have to wait until nightfall. The first thing he had to do was see Maryann.

10

HE DROVE TO THE GLIMMER MOTEL, a row of redbrick rooms at the city limits. In the lot next to the motel an old man and woman sat under an umbrella and sold watermelons from the bed of a pickup and across the street a spraypainted plywood sign announced BINGO ON TUESDAYS in front of a forgotten church. The temperature gauge spiked and the engine coughed a trail of white behind him. He left the truck running outside the motel office and when he walked in a woman and her teenage daughter sat behind the desk. The daughter unrolling curlers from her mother's hair and the sound of game show applause coming from a small television in the corner.

The woman lifted her eyes to Jack. 'You again?' she said and then her daughter opened a drawer and took out a room key attached to a small wooden block, the number 5 carved into the wood. She slid it across the counter and said don't puke in there this time or else you can clean it up yourself.

It was a short drive to Maryann. He stood at the front desk of Friendship Village Retirement Care and waited on the receptionist to finish a phone call. She then hung up and scratched her nose and asked if he needed some help.

'I'm here to see Maryann,' he said.

She looked at him cautiously. His red eyes. Dirty hands and sweat running down the sides of his face and neck.

'Do you know who I am?' he asked.

'Yes.'

'Then hand me the sign-in sheet.'

She picked up a clipboard and held it out to him. He signed his name and looked at the clock on the wall and wrote 12:20 p.m. beneath TIME IN. He handed the clipboard to her and took a deep breath. Picked a handful of tissues from a Kleenex box and wiped his face. The receptionist then turned to her computer and tapped the keyboard a few times. She gave a pensive look at the screen and then she asked Jack to sit down. A note in Maryann's file says our director needs to see you.

He moved away from the desk and scanned the great room. Separate sitting areas in the corners, sofas and loveseats in flower prints. Ferns on end tables and bouquets of fake flowers adorning coffee tables. In the middle of the room was a circle of chairs and two women sat together and shared the Clarksdale Press Register and across from them an old man stared at a small green New Testament. Residents in wheelchairs were scattered across the room and Jack wondered how many times Maryann had sat there alone and wondered where she was. Wondered where he was. He sat down on the arm of a loveseat and stared at the floor and remembered an abandoned chapel on a dirt road out on her land where she had taken him many times and told him this is where I want to be buried. Out here in the silence. A boy listening to whatever she said and then climbing in the wild magnolias and watching her walk around the woodframed chapel, its windows cracked from stormswept limbs and its sagging roof and bird nest in the corner of the small steeple. He had looked around for other headstones but found none.

From the magnolia tree he watched and he knew the look of loneliness because he had felt it so many nights in beds that were not in a home but in a house with others like him. Other lonely children who lay and wondered. He would watch her circle the chapel and he knew better than to bother her or to ask if something was wrong because it was nothing that could be explained. Only that feeling of being a singular soul amid the endless living and the countless dead with this black ground nestled against the skin of our bare feet.

He stood from the arm of the loveseat and his eyes filled. He squeezed a fist and he felt the sting in the joints of his wrist and elbow as he flexed the muscles in his hand and forearm. With the back of his hand he then wiped his eyes as a woman in a blue blazer approached him.

'I'm Linda Jones,' she said. 'The director here. You're Jack Boucher?'

'Yeah.'

'I wanted to meet with you before you go in to tell you she's not in the same room. We had to move her about two weeks ago.'

'Why'd you move her?'

Her glasses sat on the end of her nose and she took them off. 'She's getting close to the end,' she said. 'She's gotten to the point where she hardly speaks. Doesn't really know who we are. She doesn't have long and I'm sorry to have to tell you all this right before you go in. But we had no way of getting in touch with you and believe me when I say we tried.'

'Can she talk at all?'

'She talks but it's nothing coherent. She talks to people from a long time ago. Probably family members or childhood friends, which isn't unusual. It's just the way the mind works. She won't know who you are.'

'She hasn't for a long time. And I know what's coming. That's why I'm here. Can I just see her now?'

They moved into a wide corridor. The doors of resident rooms on each side and some decorated with crayon drawings of children. Suns and clouds and dogs with big ears and hearts and names and I-love-yous written in uneven capital letters. Some with out-of-season wreaths or birthday cards and some doors bare. At the end of the hallway they came to Maryann's room. The door was halfway open and a nurse was coming out. She nodded to them and then Mrs. Jones walked in first. Jack stopped in the doorway when he saw the end of the bed. Her feet only small bumps underneath the blanket and beeps from machines and the smell of a room where little moved and life waned. He tried to force her younger and happier face into his mind but before he could do it Mrs. Jones had taken him by the wrist and led him inside.

'She's sleeping,' she whispered. She let go of his wrist and asked if he wanted her to stay. Jack told her no and then she patted his shoulder and left the room.

Tubes in her nose. An IV in her arm. He looked around and nothing belonged to her. None of the furniture and none of her clothes in the closet. He moved over to the window and twisted open the blinds and the midday sun penetrated the room. Specks of dust floated like fairies and he took a chair from the corner and set it next to her bed.

He sat down and looked at her pallid eyes. Sallow cheeks. She looked hungry and weak and he wondered if she could even know what those things meant now or if her mind had chewed away at even the most basic ideas of necessity. He said her name. Thought that her eyelids twitched when he said it so he repeated it. Maryann. Maryann. No movement in her eyes but he said her name several more times because he had always liked the way it sounded. Seven days, he thought. Seven days until the house is gone and she probably has less than that. Look at her. Look at you. You couldn't have fucked up any worse.

A pitcher of water and a plastic cup were on the table next to the bed and he filled the cup. Dipped his fingertips into the water and then touched them to her dry lips. Scratchy and a pale pink as he moved his fingertip across them. He returned the cup to the table and slumped in the chair.

'I'm glad you don't know what all I've done,' he said.

He stared at Maryann and he knew what was coming for him. His own mind invaded by vast expanses of nothingness that had crept in like lava and inched their way across the green earth and burned without regard for splendor or necessity. So many fists and knees and blows to the head that could not be taken back. Could not be erased and all the damage done and feeding himself for years with whatever could medicate for the moment. For the night. And he felt the erosion but he kept feeding the whirlwind that ripped the fertile chunks of memory away. It's just the way the mind works, the woman had said. He sat up straight and leaned closer to her.

'You are beautiful,' he said and he reached for her hand. So fragile and light. The loose skin and the blue veins. He held her hand inside both of his as if it were something valuable he did not want to lose or a secret he did not want to share with the world. He tried to think of a favorite song to sing or a favorite story to tell but he was grabbed and held by now. By what he had become and by what she had become and he listened to her labored breathing and watched her body rise and fall. And then he laid his head on the bed next to her. Slipped her hand from his and pressed her palm to his ragged face.

She had always been straightforward and certain, human traits that were foreign to him as a child. He admired those qualities in the light of day but at night she grew quiet and pensive as if transformed by the dark. She became more like him. They would eat dinner and then she would make her way to the upstairs porch with a book or the newspaper and Jack would go back outside and chase fireflies or find a tree to climb until dark and then join her on the porch. By then she had set aside whatever she was reading and her eyes seemed to travel beyond the land and the stars out to a place that only she could see. At first he took her silence as a sign he had done something wrong or she was unhappy with him there but in time he began to look out toward the horizon with her, that distant realm alive in his own eyes and he had seen it in the ceiling above his bed in the group homes and seen it out of the windows of foster home bedrooms and he saw it way out there beyond this land of dust and bones where the black was as deep as heaven or hell. In the days she carried an air of optimism but by the end of their first summer together the boy had seen enough of her in the serenity of night to believe she lived with ghosts and in the mornings he sometimes expected to see their ashen footprints across the smoothworn floor.

He raised his head from the bed.

A nurse returned and saw him. Apologized and said I'll return later and he asked her to close the door. To turn off the light. Leave us alone.

11

THE FIRST TIME HE HEARD THE word lesbian was his second day of school in Clarksdale. Sixth grade. Hands shoved in his pockets and he kicked a rock in the dirt. Kids huddled in groups of three and four and some went up and down the slides and swung on swings that others believed they had outgrown. A muggy morning and the kids beginning to sweat and Jack sized up the rock and gave a hard kick. The rock skipped and bounced into the side of the merry-go-round with a clang. Four boys straddled the handlebars that crisscrossed the merry-go-round and they looked up from the sheet of notebook paper that held a crude pencil drawing of an oddshaped and naked man and woman.

'What the hell?' said the boy who held the notebook paper. He eyed Jack and Jack slid his hands from his pockets and nervously folded his arms. The four boys stared at him and then Jack shrugged his shoulders.

'I said what the hell,' the boy repeated. Louder. He had a square head and rughair. A brow stuck in perpetual meanness.

Jack walked over and picked up the rock and then turned his back to them as if he hadn't heard.

'Sissy,' the boy said. 'Sissified lesbian boy.'

Jack stopped and looked over his shoulder at the boy.

'What?'

'You heard me,' the rughaired boy said and he and the other three stepped off the merry-go-round and moved toward him and the others on the playground paused and watched. 'I said lesbian boy. Don't you live with that weird woman out in that big white house?'

'So.'

'So you ain't nothing but a lesbian boy and don't be kicking no more rocks in my direction unless you want your ass beat.'

The other kids had wandered closer now. A broken circle of curious eyes. Jack looked around as if to find empathy or encouragement and he found neither.

'You don't even know what that means,' the boy said. 'Do you?'

'I ain't talking to you.'

'You won't be able to anyhow if you got a mouthful of broken teeth.'

Jack switched the rock from one sweaty palm to the other and could not think of one word to say that could weaken what was building.

'It means your momma licks other mommas right between the legs,' another boy said and the crowd gave scattered laughter.

'She ain't my momma,' Jack said.

'That don't matter,' the rughaired boy said and he stepped face to face with Jack. Brave with the numbers behind him and shorter than Jack but his eyes hard like small stones wedged in the sockets. 'Don't matter who the hell your momma is. You're a damn lesbian boy now.'

The boy shoved Jack and he backpedaled and then tripped and fell. A small poof of dust where his rear hit the ground. Some kid yelled out kick his ass and then others hollered for a fight and still others turned away uninterested. The four boys moved toward Jack as he hustled to his feet and the rughaired boy shoved him again. Jack retreated a step. Steadied and didn't go down. But he didn't shove back.

'Fag,' one of them said.

A school bell rang from across the playground, the faint sound of salvation. A few groans in the crowd and then the sixth graders began to trudge toward the school building. The rughaired boy told him he better watch himself and he led his crew from the playground.

Jack stood there alone. As the pressure of the moment let go he felt himself begin to cry and he bit at his bottom lip to stop it. Bit so hard that it bled and when he tasted the blood he sniffed and quickly wiped his eyes with the bottom of his shirt.

'She ain't my goddamn momma,' he whispered.

That night after he and Maryann had finished drive-thru chicken and biscuits he asked her about the word lesbian. They sat at a table for two in the kitchen. She licked a fingertip and dabbed a flake of crust and stuck it in her mouth. Then she asked where he heard that word.

'At school,' he said. 'On the playground.'

She picked up the greasy takeout boxes and napkins and put them in the garbage can. She then scooped coffee and poured water into the coffee maker and turned it on and she sat down again. Tapped her fingernails on the Formica tabletop.

'Is that what you are?' he asked.

'I haven't told you what it is yet.'

'Oh.'

'Did whoever said that word tell you what it meant?'

He shrugged.

It was a small town and she had been there her entire life

but for the four years she spent at Emory University in Atlanta. A small town where her family had lived and farmed for generations and despite the great spaces in land and sky there seemed to be no secrets that could not be carried and scattered on the slightest Delta wind. She had waited and waited for the social worker to ask her such a question when she was going through the process of becoming a foster parent but to her surprise it never came. But here it was now from the boy. Who had learned of it from children who had come to this part of her life God knows how.

As she explained she could see that some things he understood and some he didn't. He sat still and watched her mouth as she spoke and when she was done she asked if he had any questions. He nodded.

'Do you know who that ugly little son of a bitch is in my class?'

'Try not to talk like that, Jack.'

'Do you?'

'What does he look like besides ugly?'

Jack tried to describe the boy. The hair tight against his head and the flat face. Maryann could only shake her head and when he was done describing the boy he told her what happened and what had been said. There were four of them and he pushed me down and then pushed me again and there wasn't nothing I could do. I don't want to go back to that school. I hate it.

Maryann stood and poured herself a cup of coffee and sat down again.

'He's going to do it again,' she said.

'I know it. That's why I'm not going.'

'You have to go. If you don't go to school your caseworker will come looking for both you and me.'

'It don't matter to me what she does.'

'And then she'll take you away from here because she'll think we don't know what we're doing together.'

'I don't care.'

'You should. Because that little jackass isn't going away. He's going to be everywhere you go. He'll look different but he'll be there. He's at school for now and then one day you'll have a job and he'll be there and he's going to get in the way when you find a girl you like and he's gonna be there in a week and in ten years and twenty years. The world never runs out of people like him and you got to figure out how to deal with it. And I can tell you one thing more. It doesn't matter what he says about me. It doesn't matter what he uses to pick a fight. Nobody has the right to call you names or push you around. Nobody.'

Brave, she wanted to say. Be brave like I could have been when I had the chance. Like I should have been.

Through the hazy blue of a fallen day she stared at the boy and wanted to touch the skin of his sunken face and form his expression into something hopeful. Transform his eyes and cheekbones and mouth into a face that would not carry such burdens. He then lifted worried eyes to her and said I know what I got to do. But I know it's going to hurt.

The next day he stood farther away from the playground and the other children. A stray from the herd that no shepherd bothered to tend. The same rock from the day before in his hands. He steadied his eyes on the four boys who again straddled the merry-go-round. The rughaired boy sighted Jack and he waved. Jack took it as some suggestion of peace and he waved back but then the rughaired boy gave the middle finger and they all laughed and then all of them waved middle fingers. A collective *fuck you* drifted across the playground and sank into Jack and he watched them no more. He turned around and stared at the cars passing along the highway at the edge of the school and thought of walking to it and sticking out his thumb. And if he had even five dollars in his pocket he would have but he had nothing but the rock.

'Lesbian boy,' the rughaired boy called as they came toward him. 'Hey lesbian boy. I saw you shoot me the bird.'

'I didn't shoot you the bird,' Jack said.

'You better keep your hands in your pockets.'

Jack didn't move.

'Right now,' said the rughaired boy. 'Put your hands in your pockets right now.'

'Just leave me alone,' Jack said.

'I was leaving you alone and then you shot the bird at us. Don't nobody do that to me. Now put your hands in your pockets.'

'Go on. I didn't do nothing to you.'

'I said shove them down or you'll get it worse than you think.'

They inched closer to him. Within reach. Jack crept back a step and he put his hands down into his pockets and as soon as they were in the rughaired boy shoved him hard in the chest with both hands. Jack shot right off his feet and he hit the ground with a flat back, the air out of his chest and he gasped as they laughed and circled him.

'I told you, lesbian boy,' the boy said. One of the others kicked him in the thigh and then they all slapped hands and walked toward the playground.

Jack caught his breath. Sat up. Then he stood and knocked the dust from his clothes and he pulled out the rock he had been clutching in his pocket. He held it gently in his fingers. And then with a long stride he hurled the rock and it surprised both him and the rughaired boy when it centered the back of his head. The boy cried out, knelt and grimaced and wondered what had happened. And then a trickle of blood ran out of a cut on his head and down his neck. He touched his head at the tender spot and then saw the crimson on his fingertips.

Jack raised his hand defiantly and this time he gave them all the finger.

And this time they all used their fists.

The boy stood in the window with his hands pressed and stared at the wobbly moon, not quite full. His eyes were swollen. So was his bottom lip. His nose hurt and his arms were bruised where he was kicked when he went to the ground and covered himself until a teacher and a coach hustled onto the scene and pushed through the crowd of children and pulled the boys away from him.

Tomorrow was Saturday. Two days before he had to go back to school. Two days to figure out what to do. He had emptied the dresser drawers and his duffel bag sat packed next to the door. He had lain down on the bed and waited until he believed Maryann was asleep and then he got up and stood in the window, trying to decide which direction to run.

Out across the moonlit acreage he imagined the river and he saw the boat coming toward him. He saw the flags and the smoke rose into the stars and the land parted and moved in waves and he saw the ghostlike figures moving across the deck and leaning over the rails of the balcony. He touched his fingertips to the window pane as the riverboat came closer and he listened and hoped to hear someone call his name and then as the black waves pushed higher and crashed upon the shores of Maryann's backyard he saw that the boat was not slowing down and it made a great mechanical roar as it pulled to the left and tossed waves against the backyard and against the house and then it was gone.

He crossed the room and picked up the duffel bag. Tucked it

under his arm. Sat down on the edge of the bed.

Out there was the world and he wanted to belong to it in some way he could not explain to himself or anyone else. And he vowed right then if he ever found the people who put him out of the car in a diaper he'd hurt them. Not the mother and father who put him out but the people because that's what they were. Sorry ass people. He had many times tried to give them faces. Stared at himself in the mirror and worked to construct the images of those who created him so he may recognize them one day. At a gas station or in a grocery store. And when he saw that moment in his mind he was grown and strong and he walked over to them and said hey it's me and before they could answer he had put fists to their faces and hands around their throats and as he imagined it now he squeezed the muscles in his forearms and his jaw clamped tightly and he felt the familiar surge of hate.

Maybe she is on my side, he thought. Unaware that Maryann had been awake below him listening to his moving about. Sitting on an antique trunk at the foot of her bed in a t-shirt and sweatpants and tennis shoes expecting him to make a run for it. She sat listening and ready, as if there would be a race to whatever answer he believed there to be on the other side of the door.

He was quiet as they drove to school. Taunting in the hallway and in the line in the cafeteria and the steady chant of lesbian boy that had been taken up now by the entire sixth grade. The rughaired boy no longer punching in places that made an immediate mark for a teacher or a principal to see but instead hitting in the lower back or in the ribs where it would take days for the bruise to show. Hitting Jack when he was standing at his locker or washing his hands and he never saw it coming.

Maryann had been to the school four more times in the past three months and she had talked with his caseworker and the school counselor. But the rughaired boy's father had shrugged it off as boys being boys and then added he didn't know people like her were allowed to have kids anyway.

When Maryann made the final turn and the school was in sight she pulled over on the side of the street. Up ahead buses were unloading and kids stood under aluminum awnings and waited for the bell to ring.

'Maybe he won't be here,' the boy said.

She didn't want to make him go in. She pulled out into the street and drove around the block and parked behind the school gym.

'Today, Jack,' she said. 'Whatever you have to do to get him to leave you alone, you do it.'

He shifted in the seat. 'I can't,' he said.

'You're going to have to.'

'I can't.'

'I know you're scared.'

'It ain't that,' he said and he began to break up. Little shakes in his chin and he put his hand across his mouth to stop it.

'What is it then?'

He choked it back. A couple of quick sucks of air and eyes squeezed tight. She let him be until he got it together and then without looking at her he said I'm afraid if I do anything bad they're going to take me away from you or you'll tell them you can't do it no more. That's what they always say. They can't do it no more and I don't want that to happen this time. I don't want to go nowhere else so I can't do nothing bad so you and them will think I ain't worth it.

She wanted to get out of the car and drop to the ground and roll around crying but that would have to wait until she got home. Instead she grabbed his hand. She held it and told him to look at her and then she promised no such thing was going to happen. No such thing, Jack. I swear.

Her words made it inside him and he seemed to pull himself up off some emotional floor. He nodded. Sat up straight. She drove around the block and pulled into the dropoff just as the bell was ringing. When he got out of the car he slammed the door in a way he hadn't done before.

A blanket of clouds and damp air and the boys and girls moved about the playground in hooded sweatshirts and denim jackets. He watched the rughaired boy in the monotone morning and waited for the right time.

The right time came when the rughaired boy and his friends moved to the slide. They stood together at the ladder and slapped at one another and then one pulled a tennis ball from his coat pocket. The boys spread out and tossed the ball to one another and then the rughaired boy told one of them to stand out in front of the slide with the ball. He did and the others took turns climbing the ladder and going down the slide and trying to catch the ball as they raced toward the bottom.

Jack crept closer to them until he was near enough to make a run. He watched while the rughaired boy waited his turn and he felt as if he were burning inside as he began to flex his fingers. The rughaired boy ascended the steps of the ladder and Jack moved. One step toward the slide and then another and then just as the rughaired boy sat down at the top Jack broke into a run and his bottom foot hit the slide and in two great strides he was to the top and his fist went into the face of the rughaired boy. The boy's head snapped back and then Jack hit him again and this time his body tumbled in a slack flip and flopped onto the mulch covered ground.

It happened quickly and confused the others but he was not done. He jumped from the slide and then knelt over the rughaired boy and with one hand he held him by the ear and with the other he busted the boy's face into snot and blood. Others began to shout and adults raced toward the playground and as they pried Jack away and dragged him toward the school building he was screaming in a fierce and shrieking voice, I hope you're fucking dead.

Round Two

12

When Jack finally raised his head from Maryann's bed the day was gone. An imprint of the quilt matted on the side of his face. A nurse had turned on a lamp while he slept and outside a thick and windless rain had settled in and drenched the Delta.

He slid the quilt up across her chest and said I'll be back.

He then drove to the house. The rain was light but the western sky remained stonegray and menacing and promised more to come. Jack pulled into the drive and parked next to the potter's barn. He picked up the dead body, the tarp slick and slippery but he managed to wrestle it into the truck bed.

He stood there in the graying night with his hands on his hips and he stared out across the plain, tried to imagine what he would say to Big Momma Sweet. His reckless nature told him to run. But he was beyond that. They had begun to come after him and would continue and he knew he was living in the immediacy of have to. You have to make some deal to get her to call off the dogs. You have to sell the antiques you put in storage or rob a convenience store or do something to find a few thousand dollars to make her believe you'll come up with the rest. You have to survive because Maryann is fighting to survive. He felt the raindrops on his face and then he imagined her there in the bed, a nurse having turned off the lamp and the room falling dark and the beeps from the machine and her deepset eyes and the bottomless dark of her mind that all her memories had fallen into and though he knew she belonged to another world now he somehow believed she had waited for him. She had fought to keep her heart beating and her eyes opening and closing and opening again because she somehow knew he would be there when the moment came. And I am here, he thought. There is nowhere left to hide so you better hope like hell there is one deal left to make.

It had begun a hundred years ago as a trading camp for travelers up and down the Mississippi River. Stables and a square hut sitting atop and anchored to railroad ties that held it in place when the waters rose. The camp along a thin strip of river vein that reached inland and was nestled in a clump of hardwoods. Out beyond the trees a field of sunflowers bloomed in the heat of summer and surrounded an old graveyard with leaning headstones covered in black grime.

Now a huddle of shacks stood around what was left of the original square hut. Out behind the shacks there was a metal structure with only a roof, the width and length of a high school gymnasium, where Big Momma Sweet housed her collection of payoffs. On one side cars, tractors, four-wheelers, trucks, cattle trailers. When they owed and didn't have the cash, they offered and she took. On the other side of the barn four posts had been driven into the ground. The posts eight feet high. A chainlink fence wrapped the four posts in a shaky square and bleachers swiped from a junior high football field sat on two sides of the square. This was where they fought.

A cinderblock building stood at the edge of the barn. Stout

and rectangular. A thick door on the side, locked with three industrial padlocks. Only one window and it was in the front. Iron bars covering it. The cinderblocks gray and written across the window in black spraypaint were the words THE PO HOUSE. This was where the bets were made on the nights of the fights. Where bulky men and serious dogs stood on guard as the money flowed.

Electric light glowed from the shack windows in the rainy night. In the shack closest to the muddy road a one man show kicked a drum and bent an E chord while a cluster of rowdy women held each other up and danced and hollered for him to play Red Rooster. Everydamnbody knows how to play Red Rooster and we ain't got all night. He stopped in the middle of the song and said what the hell you got to do if you ain't got all night? One of them said you ain't nobody's momma and a bottle of gin passed between them and he was sick of listening to it so he played what they asked for. They all hooted and one fell out drunk. Rain beat against the tin roof and the women shook their wide hips and slapped at whatever ass was within reach.

In another shack the cards were dealt. Three round tables surrounded by folding chairs and each chair filled. Coolers stacked with ice and beer nestled between the tables. A smokefilled room and a man with a thick neck and square head sat in the corner with the money. A pitbull laying in wait on the floor next to him, chained to the wall. Two other men with muscles and scars milled around the tables watching for slips or counting or any other twitch that would move them into action.

A four-room cabin stood behind the shacks on ten-foot stilts and watched over all. In the front room Big Momma Sweet sat on a stool smoking a pipe and sharpening a knife. Her meaty hands holding the bone handle and slowly sliding the blade across a whetstone. She held the knife up to a lowhanging bulb and squinted. Satisfied she set the knife on the table next to the others. A collection of knives she had taken off those who emptied their pockets for the grace of another day and others she found at gun and knife shows. Relics from the Civil War. Both World Wars. A double-edge blade with a swastika carved in the steel handle. Knives with handles made from elephant tusks and deer antlers and California redwood. Knives she kept sharp and shiny and allowed their glimmer to say much of what she wanted to say.

She rubbed her hands together and stood from the stool. A husky woman and her wild graying afro made a strange shadow against the paneled wall of the cabin. She plopped down into a recliner and sucked on the pipe. A long flowery housecoat wrapping her big arms and legs. She laid back her head and let the smoke drain from her lips and she listened to the rain and the muffled rhythm of the blues and the cries of the rambunctious women who moved along with it.

'You want something, Big Momma?' Ern asked. He stood next to the window and kept an eye out for headlights coming or going.

'Naw,' she said.

'Don't look like it's gonna stop raining.'

'It ain't. I can tell it in my kneebone.'

'I wish I had a dollar for everything your kneebone claimed to know.'

He moved over and took the stool and set it next to her. Cracked his knuckles and then ran his hand across his shaved head. 'What you think happened to Skelly?'

'There ain't no telling.'

'You think he was lying?'

'I think Skelly would tell you he was having dinner with Jesus if he thought it'd get himself a little more time.'

'You want me to go look for him?' Ern asked.

'No. Skelly can't handle Jack. We both know that. Jack's the one we got to look for.'

'Word's out.'

'Word is out but I count two in Natchez who couldn't get a hold of him and now Skelly.'

Big Momma got up from the recliner. In a silver bin in the corner she had her own beer and ice and she opened a can of Budweiser. Set the pipe in the windowsill and saw headlights and said here comes somebody else.

'Games are full up,' Ern said.

'Go on out and see. If there ain't no seats send whoever it is in there with the women.'

This had been her spot for a dozen years and every walk of life had sat at her tables. Smoked her weed. Drank her beer. Bought her women. Men in coats and ties and men with badges and men with wives and men with big bankrolls and men playing with social security checks. Men who knew the rules before they got there and men who didn't ask any questions. But she had not gotten her reputation by being lazy and nothing rolled into her place without one of her grunts going out and giving them the okay. Not if she had seen the vehicle fifty times. Not if it was her own kinfolk. So Ern walked out and down the stairs and into the rain to see who it was and the truck slid to a stop in the slick mud.

Big Momma watched from the window and heard the voices. Saw the headlights go black and the truck door slam and then saw Ern hustling up the steps. He came in the cabin and said it's him.

She didn't ask who. Only watched as Jack walked through the rainy night with a rolled blue tarp slung over his shoulder. He struggled up the stairs and followed Ern inside and then let out a great huff as he dropped the tarp onto the floor.

'Here's your boyfriend,' he said and he bent over with his hands on his knees. Trying to catch his breath.

'Get that wet shit outta here,' Ern said and he took a step toward Jack.

Big Momma drew on the pipe. Walked a slow circle around the tarp and then she adjusted her bra against her big bosom. 'That don't look like your money to me,' she said.

'I don't have the damn money. I did before this piece of shit got in the way,' he said and then he reached down and grabbed the edge of the tarp. He yanked it and the tarp unrolled and Skelly's mangled body flopped onto the cabin floor.

'What the hell you think you're doing?' Ern said.

'Look,' Jack said. He rolled Skelly on his stomach and put his bootheel on the branded dollar sign on the back of his neck.

'Don't nobody give a goddamn about that,' Ern said and he snatched Jack by the arm. 'You just walked up in here and tossed a dead man on the floor?'

Jack tried to yank his arm away but Ern held tight and said you better remember where you are.

'Turn him loose,' Big Momma said. 'He ain't never had no manners.'

Ern let go of Jack's arm and the men stood close. Their noses nearly touching.

'Back off,' she said. 'Both of y'all. Right now.'

Each man took a step back. And then Jack pointed his bootheel again at the brand on the back of Skelly's neck.

'You think I don't know how it got there?' she said. 'But I guess you're in luck. It's raining tonight. Can't get the fire going till it stops.'

'I'm just showing because you're not doing that shit to me.'

'You ain't the boss,' Ern said.

Big Momma shushed Ern. Took a box of matches from her housecoat pocket and struck one and held it to the pipe. A yellow flame rose as she puffed and outside the thunder rumbled across the rainsoaked land.

'I can't figure out if you're getting braver or dumber,' she said. 'But you have made the kind of entrance you ain't in no position to be making.'

She nodded to Ern and he disappeared out the back door and then she told Jack to come on. He followed her out the front door of the cabin and they stood together on the covered deck.

'I had the money. Every nickel.'

'So where is it?'

'I lost it when that little motherfucker pulled a knife on me when I was giving him a ride. Truck turned over and by the time I came to it was gone. That's all I know. Look at my goddamn eyes.'

'You look like a pile of shit bricks.'

'I know it.'

'And you don't look capable no more.'

'Capable of what?'

She turned to him and poked her finger into his cheek. 'Not a single damn thing.' Down below a shack door opened and two men followed Ern out and over to the cabin. The three men climbed the stairs and then stood behind Jack on the other end of the deck.

'Most I ever let anybody get into with me was about ten grand. Know where he's at?'

Jack turned around and looked at the men behind him and he imagined them dragging him into the night. Dropping him into a muddy hole. 'I could probably figure it out,' he said.

'Only reason I let you get so deep is cause you made me some money when you was worth a shit. I ain't never seen nobody fix a fight good as you. Even when everybody knew it was a setup it always came off different from what they was expecting. That was a good trick, but I don't figure you got any more tricks left. Or else you wouldn't have let that worm in there get to you.'

'What kind of price you got on me?'

'The kind that'll get you chased down no matter where you go.'

A roll of thunder and the storm came stronger now. The wind pushed the rain beneath the covering in soft sprays and then Jack felt a sting in the back of his neck. The first sign that the bad one was coming. He put his hand to his neck and rubbed but the pain crawled. Up into his head and over behind his right ear. It had been ten hours since he washed the pills down the drain and it was coming now, like he expected it to but not right now. Not goddamn now, he thought and he shoved his fingers into his neck and squeezed his eyes shut and said little prayers of hope that it would hold off until he could find a way out of this place. But it kept crawling, past his ear and up into his eyes and he gritted his teeth and dropped to a knee. Moved his hands to the sides of his head and pressed until his hands shook.

'Quit playing,' she said and then she told Ern to get the shovel and that other thing. He left them and she told the other two to wait right here. She reached down and took Jack by the arm. Helped him to his feet and led him inside and then he went down to both knees. Doubled over with his head on the floor and his body writhed as he fought the fire in his head. She took a beer from the bin and then she opened up a table drawer and took out a bag of pills.

'Get up,' she said.

He wrestled with it. Raised his head off the floor. His eyes squeezed shut but he opened them when he heard the beer open. She picked a red pill and a blue pill from the bag. Placed them in the palm of her open hand and extended her hand to him. He shook his head but she did not withdraw, she only held her hand there patiently until he gave in and moved his mouth closer to her hand and when he opened his mouth she dropped them in. She gave him the beer and he drank and swallowed and then she dropped the bag into her housecoat pocket.

'I keep waiting for something different from you but you're more fucked up every time I see you,' she said. She moved to the window and watched the storm. 'And you ain't got no damn money cause if you did you'd be giving it to me. You ain't got nothing to get no money with. Mr. Bank Man comes out here sometimes to get rubbed on and he says you can't get no more from that place that woman gave you. I believe you maybe had it. I heard you was running pretty hot down in Natchez. But had ain't the same thing as have.'

Big Momma Sweet then moved over to the table and picked up one of the knives. A long straight blade. A stainless steel handle. She held the pipe in her mouth and slid the blade between the rough skin of her fingertips. Ern returned and stood in the doorway. A shovel in one hand and the branding iron in the other. Jack put his hands on the arm of the sofa and raised to his feet. He held his hand over his eyes as if shielding from the sun and looked at her. At the men and the shovel and the branding iron.

'Turn the iron on, Ern,' she said.

Against the wall was a short and square safe Ern had found sunk down in the riverbank. He leaned the shovel against the wall and then reached inside the open door and lifted out a clothes iron and he plugged it into the wall. He set the clothes iron on top of the safe and pressed the brand against it.

'Don't really need no fire,' Big Momma said. 'We long since figured that out.'

Jack lowered his hand from his eyes and said I can get you paid.

'Untrue.'

'I can. I've got some more stuff I can sell. A whole shed full of furniture I took out of the house.'

'Listen to yourself.'

'I swear to God.'

'It's too late,' she said.

'Goddamn it,' he said and he walked a small circle. He pressed at his temples with his middle fingers hoping to neutralize the pain long enough to get out of this.

'What's wrong with him?' Ern asked.

'Nothing more than usual,' she said.

He pressed his temples harder and harder. Bent over and up again. He moved to the sofa and leaned against it and the pain held steady with the pressure.

'Just give me a day or two,' he mumbled. 'I won't go anywhere.'

'Nah. You won't. But you also won't have my money so I figure the only way for me to get it back is the oldfashioned way.'

He moved his hands from his head. Squinted at her and said I can't do that no more.

'How come?'

'Can't you see me? My damn head will explode.'

'You been fighting, I heard.'

'Those weren't real fights and you know it. Not like you want to do. And I was full of dope.'

'You can get full of dope again,' she said and she held up the bag of pills. 'And I think you will because your choice is this. Fight or don't fight. You might get hurt with the first option. You *will* get hurt and worse from the second.'

'I'm not going to fight. Tomorrow I'll bring you whatever

money I got and I'll figure out a way to get you the rest. The only reason I'm here now is to stay with Maryann.'

'Until one of you dies.'

'If you want to put it that way.'

She snapped her fingers and the men were on Jack. He swung wild but only grazed the top of Ern's forehead and then they had his arms pinned and Ern busted Jack again and again in his ribcage while he screamed from the scorching pain in his head and neck. Ern cracked him once across the jaw and the blood came from his mouth and he slumped in the men's grasp. Big Momma said hold it right there and Ern stepped back.

She removed the pipe from the corner of her mouth and set it down on the table with the knife. Ern grabbed the branding iron from the top of the safe and the men let Jack down to his knees, but they kept his arms held behind him.

She strolled across the room. Took the brand from Ern. She stood back from Jack and studied him as if he were some creature she had never seen before. Then she moved close and knelt beside him. Leaned her face close to Jack and said where do you want it. The blood trailed from his mouth and dripped onto the scarred plank floor. His breath came in small huffs of desperation and she was a blurred figure, his eyes watery and unfocused from the pain behind them and he did not answer and only dropped his head.

She twirled the dollar sign under his nose.

'Hold his head,' she said.

The men held his arms tighter and Ern wrapped his strong hands around Jack's ears. She moved the iron to the side of his neck, a slither of smoke past the corner of his eye and he began to struggle again. His eyes wide as Ern pressed his hands against the sides of Jack's head and the iron inching closer. A dribble of spit and blood down the side of his mouth and neck and then he let go. The tension falling from his body. His eyes to the floor. And he whispered. Stop. Please stop. I'll do whatever you want.

Big Momma paused. Leaned her mouth close and spoke into his ear in a low, lustful voice. I wish you knew how bad I want to put you out of your misery. How bad I want to let them take you out and set the dogs on you. I wish you were the Jack I used to know but you ain't no more. But for one night you will be. She held the iron in her thick fingers and eased it closer to his neck. Take this with you she said and she touched the edge of the hot brand to the skin. His eyes coming alive and he jerked but the men held him and she pressed the heat against his skin until she had made a sliver of a burn.

She inched the branding iron away. Watched the seared strip of skin turn red. A new scar to join the others. She then reached into her housecoat pocket and removed the bag of red and blue pills and she grabbed Jack's hair and raised his head. Set her eyes close to his and said I don't give a shit if your head explodes or if you catch on fire. You got one more fight in you cause that's the only way I'm gonna get what I need out of you. I don't want to hear no more fairy tales about getting me some money now and getting me some money later. You know it's bullshit and what's worse than that is I know it's bullshit. You ain't no good dead. You ain't much good alive either. But you're gonna fight. That little burn on the side of your neck ain't nothing. It'll be the full brand next time. That little headache you think you got now ain't nothing. Screw me again and you'll find out what hurt is and then after I'm done you'll help feed this sweet land of ours with your sorry skin and bones.

She looked up at the men holding him and they twisted his arms back further. He cried out in pain and she let him scream until she was satisfied and she told them to let go. Jack collapsed on the floor. Facedown next to Skelly, his expression frozen in pain and anguish for all of eternity and his eyes halfopen and looking at Jack as if to say you will be here soon. Jack gasped in agony and sucked in the wet and sour smell of death and he covered his mouth and nose with both hands and rolled away from the body.

Big Momma dropped the bag of pills on the floor next to him and then she stood. Straightened her housecoat across her bosom and belly and she patted her afro. 'What's today, Ern?' she asked.

'Wednesday, Big Momma.'

'Sounds to me like Friday night would be a good night for Jack's comeback. We'll take tomorrow to spread the word. I just hope you ain't dead by then. What you think, Jack?'

He answered her with hard coughs.

'Go somewhere and take those pills. You better come back out here ready to put on a show.'

'And don't try to run nowhere,' Ern said.

'He ain't running. That'd be the same as putting a gun to his own head. He can't sit and watch his momma die if he runs away neither. Now get this piece of shit out of here,' she said and the men reached to grab him again. But she clapped her hands at them and said that's not what I'm talking about. She grabbed the shovel that leaned against the wall and she dropped it on the floor next to Jack, the shovel clanging and knocking against his back. And then she told Jack to get up. Wipe your own blood off my floor. And then get that trash you brought in here out of my house. Go put it in the ground. Deep where them damn dogs can't dig it up.

13

HE DRAGGED SKELLY OUT INTO THE night. Out beyond the graveyard and into the sunflowers that were beaten down by the rain. The storm had shifted again and the rain was straight and strong and slapping against the wet earth and he sloshed through the bottomless night like some creature returning wounded to its den.

He dropped the shovel next to the tarp and sank down in the mud. The drone of the storm and he imagined the rain to be some lubricant for his bones or a healing shower that would wash his hurt and sins away. He began to rock and there was thunder and he imagined himself sinking into the earth in a slow and peaceful draw as if returning to the nothing from which he had come. And as he imagined the great fingers of the world reaching up from the mud and pulling him under he gave himself up to the notion he had rejected his entire life. I don't need help and whatever you got I can take it and there will be no prayers. This idea of clemency he had fought with anger and deadened with pills and supported with stubbornness. The storm bore down and he wrapped his arms around himself like he had done as a child when there was no one else to do it and for the first time in his life he called out for help.

He cried out into the black and flowing night to whoever or whatever might exist in this cavernous expanse of space and sky, cried out to the mother of nature and the breath of the world or to the idea of some infinite thing that could pull him up from his depths. He cried out for love and forgiveness and he begged for help. Please help me. Please. He dropped his arms and his head back and the water washing the blood down his neck and chest and washing the mud from his outstretched hands and he cried and called out with the despair of a forgotten child.

After rising from his knees and after burying Skelly. After making it to the truck cab and swallowing two pills and after tires spinning and slipping along the slushy road. After finding pavement and making it to the liquor store and after paying the frowning clerk with bills dripping with brown water and after making it to the motel room he stripped off his wet and mudcovered clothes and toweled his hair and stared at himself in the mirror and tried to find which muscles would give him the best chance of surviving one last fight. His body still lean and his shoulders still hard and his fists like stones but he saw only the body of a man who seemed to have been thrown down a flight of stairs and then dragged up to the top and thrown down them again. For years. He had begged for help as he knelt in the pit of night but he only saw deliverance in the pint bottles and pills she had given him and the empty room.

He turned off the lights and sat down naked on the ribbed carpet. Shades of blueblack across the room. His back against the bed. He unscrewed the cap of the whiskey. He swallowed a pill and he drank and the lightning flashed behind the curtain and through the thin walls he heard the racket and howls of either a wrestling match or fornication. The bottle to his mouth and whiskey trails down his chin and he didn't let the bottle touch the ground until it was empty and then he slung it against the wall. The bottle didn't break but bounced and he crawled over to it and slung it again and it shattered. The noise from the other side paused at the crash but then cranked up again with more ferocity than before.

The room suddenly became strange to him and he held out his arms to steady himself. Another snap of lightning and he wanted to escape, stepping on broken glass as he crossed the room and opened the door. Naked in the rain and moving along the strip of motel rooms and calling out for Maryann because that was the only name he could remember and beating on doors and windows with limp fists. Lights coming on and eyes between separated curtains and threats shouted as locks clicked and reclicked. He stumbled and fell and stayed on his hands and knees. His forehead down to the concrete and all dark and wet and then the four hands on him. Lifting and dragging him to his room and throwing him on the bed and a voice commanding him to stay your ass right there or I'll call the law and then the door slamming.

He sat up in the bed. Got to his feet and threw drunken punches into the air. Shifted his hips and lazily ducked and dodged. Kicked and gave a forearm and then grabbed the imaginary head of the imaginary opponent and delivered a headbutt that shattered the imaginary nose. Another array of punches and he lost his balance and fell against the table and crashed into the wall. The bottle on the table toppling and falling into his lap. He raised a shaking hand to the curtain and pushed it back. The water ran down the large window in crooked silver streaks and he opened the new bottle and drank.

His mind spun in circles of memory. Flashes of a whiteframed house and a shutter blown loose in a winter storm and the clap clap clap of the shutter banging against the house in the cold wind. A woman on her porch swing and another woman in the dark corner of a bar and a busted face against a dirt floor and the hot and blinding sun of a day spent catching frogs along a soggy creek bank. Flashing lights of the great floors of casinos and the cross smile of a slickhaired dealer and a baseball in the air and a boy in a red uniform trying to run under it. In his drunk and drugged stupor his life passed by in ghosts and apparitions and he searched for something specific to hold on to but his mind flowed like a river that both brought visions to him and carried them away. His head fallen against the window pane and his eyes out into the storm and the only thing he knew was that he had once been a boy and then he had become a hitchhiker through his own life. He stared at the silver trails of rain against the window and from somewhere far behind his eyes came the shrill cry of a hawk.

14

ANNETTE COULD NOT SLEEP. THE RAIN slapping at the camper from all sides. A lantern on the small table. Sitting in the chair next to the table with her knees drawn up under her chin and the orange tip of a cigarette moving in the dim light and the claustrophobia of the limited space that she only felt when the weather turned nasty. The door was locked and the window above the table opened a few inches to let out the cigarette smoke. Next to the lantern a red pen she had been using to draw stars on the palm of her hand.

She had taken a shoebox from the tiny closet and set it on the table. And then she had placed the bulky envelope Baron had given her on top of the shoebox as if to create a witness stand where she could coerce the money into giving her the truth. For the last hour she had been talking to it. Explaining to it that she knew it was there for a reason. I know you have a story. We all have a story but some are better than others and you and me both know there's a tale twisted up in you. She would lean forward in the chair and put her mouth close to the envelope and pronounce her words with deliberation. She would pace around the small space waving her hands and tossing her shoulders, creating a nonverbal animation she hoped would trick the money into raising its head from the envelope flap and confessing.

She tried different tones of voice and emotional pleas and when the envelope would not talk back, she would lay her hands on it. Hold the cigarette in the side of her mouth and squint from the smoke up into her eyes and then whisper a prayer of coincidence from her pursed lips. We are bound by the same things, O God. You have delivered a message with strength, O God. You have delivered an answer to a great question, O God.

But what the hell is it?

For an hour she smoked and listened to the rain and prayed over the envelope and talked to the envelope and waited for answers and there was no thunder. No lightning. No rattle from the natural world that she felt like she needed to drive her toward a conclusion. Spiritual or otherwise. The storm gained strength as the night dragged on and her frustration escalated with the wind and the rain. And then there was thunder and then there was lightning and she smoked cigarette after cigarette while this unmistakable symbol of fate sat silently on top of the shoebox and as the wind began to rock the small camper she pleaded for the envelope to say something. Anything. And then she had to get out.

She opened the camper door and walked into the storm. Held her long black and purple hair up with her hands and felt the cool rain against her neck. An instant relief in the dark summer night. And in the storm she let go of her frustration and realized that the answer would come from the envelope when it was time. There was always a time for what was supposed to happen in her theological world and she felt guilty for trying to pressure the envelope into giving itself away, but she did not hold on to the guilt for long. There will be no more questions, she said into the night. No more questions. No more inquisitions. She twisted her hair up on top of her head and she closed her eyes. Just do what you have always done, she thought. Look and listen and be ready for the answer when it comes.

He slouched through the thunderstorm with his back bent and a coat draped over his head. A dark humpbacked shadow. The carnival workers hidden away in their vehicles playing cards or smoking weed or rocked to sleep by the rain. But Ricky Joe was milling through the night. Moving from one residence to the next in the mobile home park. Pulling on car door handles and finding some open and taking what he liked. His pockets filling with their spare change and random dollar bills and cigarette lighters. Headphones and checkbooks. A watch and CDs and a pair of running shoes.

When the cars and trucks would give no more he stepped onto their porches, his footfalls silenced beneath the rhythm of the rain. He reached into mailboxes that hung next to front doors and he studied bicycles to see if they had pawnshop value. Sometimes he stood close to a window when he could see the light from within and he tried to listen to what was on television or eavesdrop on the conversation of the two faceless voices but the thrum of the storm would give no clarity.

At the mobile homes where there were no cars and no lights he turned door handles but had no luck. And then he began to creep around the backsides, up onto porches or into aluminum storage sheds. In the sheds he came across nail guns and lawnmowers and cordless drills. He took a couple of drills and handheld saws and marked his memory for where to return to collect the rest in the coming days as the carnival entertained and the caravan stayed put, taking a little at a time, a steady stream of theft that would keep extra cash in his pocket from his pawnshop deliveries. Satisfied with his first haul he headed back toward the caravan, sloughing across a sodden field on the edge of the park. His pockets full and an armload of tools and he felt a satisfaction in the cover of the storm when he heard the pop.

He paused. Moved again. And then another pop. This time when he looked he saw the flash of light from the end of the rifle. A tiny bright burst. The thunder roared as he heard another pop and saw another flash and he dropped his loot and ran and in the morning the residents would find their belongings in a scattered trail across the wet field.

But the humpbacked shadow was not finished. He saw the light on inside her eggshaped camping trailer and he sloshed across the parking lot and stood next to the window. His clothes heavy with the rain and his hair matted against his head and the tip of his nose rubbing against the glass. One eye into the slit between the curtains. Watching as she brushed the tangles out of her wet hair. Watching as she peeled off her wet clothes. Watching as she sat in a chair with only a towel draped across her lap, her lips moving as if she was talking to herself. His one eye leaving her mouth and then sliding from one tattoo to the next, hypnotized by her damp, naked body. Never noticing the envelope on the table, the object of her conversation.

15

ANNETTE STOOD WITH HER HANDS ON her hips as the carnival rose across the widereaching stretch of concrete. Whatever was there had been leveled and forgotten piles of cinderblocks and rebar and air-conditiong ducts were spread across the lot in small monuments of deconstruction. An odd coolness in the air from the big storm that had blown across the Delta in the night and puddles in the sunken spaces of broken concrete. Birds standing and stabbing in the puddles with tiny beaks. Baron had scribbled the layout for the rides and games and concessions down on a paper towel and he walked the lot and directed the workers and the carnival was erected around the piles of debris. The concession stand right in the middle. The tents for the rigged games in a staggered line over to the right. The rides going up where they could find enough consistent space. The Tilt-A-Whirl and Tornado and Slingshot. A maze of cracked mirrors and a carousel with missing horses. Bumper cars and a tiny racetrack where toddlers sat on stumpy elephants and zebras and held on as they motored in a clunky circle. At the back end was the Ferris wheel which was not much higher than a young oak but its pink lights shined in the night and gave a view across the carnival and made children believe they were somewhere near the clouds. Out behind the ticket booth were inflatable castles for jumping and a tall slide where children sat on potato sacks to zoom to the bottom.

The workers moved about with their shirts off and with cigarettes and Annette watched as her stage was being put together behind the concession stand. Baron kept her in the middle of the festivities so the carnival goers could catch her from all sides.

Coming and going from the games or the kiddie rides or as they staggered and rubbed knots on their heads after the maze of mirrors. Peeking over their shoulders as they bought popcorn or footlong corndogs. Her circular stage with surrounding spotlights and its own speakers so she could play her own music. A curtain wrapped the stage and behind the curtain she stretched and rubbed her body with baby oil so that she would shine in the spotlights. A string of different colored bikinis hung on a strip of PVC pipe. A braided velvet cord roped off the stage and held spectators back for twenty feet in every direction and if you wanted to get on the other side of the rope and gaze more closely at the tattooed woman it cost five dollars.

But that was only the teaser. Once inside the rope a poster board sat on an easel at the side of the stage and showed six images. For ten dollars you could choose the image that you wanted to find on her body. And then the attendant allowed you up the steps and onto the stage where you sat down in a chair. The curtain closed and the clock began ticking on your own personal two minutes with the slick and sensual woman who would turn and bend however you asked her to while you searched for the image selected. If you found the image the prize was a crisp one hundred dollar bill. A crisp one hundred dollar bill that didn't exist and wasn't necessary as none of the images was on Annette's body in one form. Once the two minutes ran out she would then contort her body in such a way as to join tattoos and form the image. Her calf and her forearm pressed together formed a fleur de lis. The front of her forearm and the side of her thigh made a hammer and sickle. A calf and a wrist gave a blackbird on a grapevine. When she was done she gave a devilish grin and opened the curtain to the wide-eyed faces who had succumbed to the erotic wonder of what might have transpired behind the deep red cover.

A dirty trick like all the dirty little tricks of the carnival but not one that had ever been complained about as it was considered ten dollars well spent. Some even came back for seconds and thirds, not for the chance at a crisp one hundred dollar bill but instead for the pure delight of directing her into the longlegged pose of choice.

Now she was bored. After a year on the stage, after a year of the gawks and mumbled insinuations as she turned and bent, after a year of men and sometimes women waiting for her after the show was over and making lonely and lustful pitches for her time and more. She watched the workers assemble the stage and she wondered if she would be on it when the carnival opened that night. Or if she would be rolling down the highway with the money Baron had given her for safekeeping. Not waiting until they could deliberate over it further. Just going. He has been good to me but I've been good for his wallet, she thought. Good only takes you so far. She had spent most of the night talking to the money and listening for the money to talk back. To make its purpose or her purpose more clear. But she was still listening without an answer.

She wandered toward the concession stand where her stage would be. She held a cup of coffee that had long since cooled and she poured it out. And then Ricky Joe eased next to her. He had finished adjusting the chains and topping off the oil levels of the engines that propelled the rides and he wiped his hands on a rag. A bead of sweat dripped from the tip of his pointed nose and she frowned when she smelled him.

'What?' she said.

'How come your hands don't never get dirty?' he asked. When he grinned he showed the gap from a missing bottom tooth and his long lank hair was damp with sweat.

'My hands get dirty. Just not the same way as yours.'

'That ain't true.'

'What do you want?'

'Nothing,' he said. 'Just talking.'

'I don't have time, Ricky Joe.'

'I was just wondering. About the other night.'

'What about it?'

'That wreck out there.'

'What about it?'

'I saw you and the bossman walking around out there.'

'So?'

'Just seemed like you two was out there pretty long.'

'Talk to Baron if you got some bright idea,' she said.

'Maybe I will.'

She walked across the lot and found Baron and told him she would be back later. He asked her where she was going but she only shrugged her shoulders.

'You figured out what to do with it yet?' he asked.

'No. But Ricky Joe acts like he knows something.'

'What makes you think that?'

'The way he was just talking to me. And looking at me.'

Baron folded the paper towel with the layout scribble and stuck it in the pocket of his shirt. Then he searched the grounds for Ricky Joe and found him, Ricky Joe turning away as Baron's eyes caught his.

'He knows how to work on about any kind of engine but other than that he's dumb as shit,' Baron said.

'That's the part that worries me about him. Dumb don't think it through. Dumb just does it.'

'Me and you will sit down tonight and decide if it stays or if it goes. You look a little spooked.'

'It was probably just the storm kept me up thinking.'

'When you don't sleep it can make you paranoid,' he said.

'When you don't sleep and there's thunder and lightning and an envelope of cash under your pillow found at the scene of a wreck with a dead man, that'll also make you paranoid.'

Baron took out a pack of cigarettes and tapped them in the palm of his hand. 'Relax,' he said. 'Forget about it for now.'

'Is it going to bother you if you look in whatever newspaper they got here tomorrow and see a fat envelope full of money has been dropped at the door of the Baptist church?'

'It will if you don't wait until we decide on it together.'

'You want it back. Don't you?'

'I told you, we'll figure it out this evening after the carnival shuts down. Have a few beers and a few cigarettes and we'll see if it's still driving us crazy after that. But it'll be gone tomorrow. If you get the feeling Ricky Joe is sniffing around then it won't be long before a few others are too.'

The first night of the carnival was always slow. And something of a test run as the popcorn machine or the sound system or any number of other things that needed electricity let it be known that they had suffered too many bumps in the road and required attention. But the carnival tents and lights signaled to those passing in their cars or riding on school buses that at least for a little while something new had been inserted into the familiar landscape.

Annette did her job. Strutted across her stage. Turned and

twisted under the spotlights. Smiled the way she was supposed to smile to get them to pay. But her mind was not on those who paid the fee to sit close to her. Studying the curves in her hips and the bend in her back. Asking her questions she would not answer. She could not keep her eyes from wandering across the grounds. Watching the other workers as they sold hot dogs or provided warped basketballs to shoot at warped rims or as they walked past her and stared. She kept her eyes on them from her perch and Ricky Joe kept coming and going. And he glared at her as he passed along the tent row of games or as he moved between the concession stand and the ticket booth. Their eyes meeting in a queer exchange of the unspoken. The distrustful. When the carnival closed for the night she did not sit in the lawn chair with Baron and drink a beer and she left a note on the dashboard of his Suburban that because she hadn't slept the night before she was going to bed. She did not speak to anyone else. She went directly to her trailer and locked the door behind her. Pulled the money from beneath a short stack of shoeboxes in the small cabinet below her bed. And she sat up until deep into the night with an ashtray on the mattress and she smoked and listened for footsteps in the dark.

16

JACK HAD TWO DAYS TO PREPARE for the fight. And he lost one in the motel room. He woke up sick and he stayed sick all day. Vomiting and coughing. Taking more red pills and more blue pills and drinking more whiskey to rid him of the sickness of taking too many pills and drinking too much whiskey. He only opened the door twice to get some air and he kept his eyes closed while he did because the daylight hurt. Then he would go back inside and crawl into bed. Sleep some and then wake and vomit again and drink water from a plastic cup. Run cold water onto a washrag and hold it to his fresh cuts and bruises from Big Ern and from the truck wreck. Press the cold rag against the burn Big Momma Sweet had put on his neck as a preview. He was hungry but he knew he could not eat. He washed his clothes in the bathtub, the dried mud flaking off and clogging the drain. He hung them over the shower curtain rod to dry and then he was back into the bed and there was only tomorrow.

17

THE NEXT MORNING ANNETTE UNHITCHED THE camping trailer from the pickup and she drove into town. The money with her. Ricky Joe followed in his El Camino, staying far enough behind so that she didn't notice. Passing sale lots lined with tractors and farm equipment. A co-op where a forklift raised and lowered pallets of fertilizer and feed. Car repair and tire repair and a pawnshop with a motorcycle sitting out by the road with the front tire missing and propped on a stack of bricks, the sign across the handlebars reading AS IS.

She was looking for somewhere to sit. Somewhere to pull out a chair and drink coffee and stare at the morning. She crossed the railroad tracks and came to the gathering of city blocks of downtown Clarksdale. At a bus station a pregnant woman sat on a bench outside with her arms folded across the top of her stomach. A table covered with books sat on the sidewalk outside a secondhand bookstore and a woman rocked in a rocking chair next to the table waving to passersby. Annette drove slowly past empty banks. Empty department stores. Shells of yesterday. But she found life at a coffee shop on the corner. Doors painted a royal blue and a rainbow across the window on one side and a Les Paul guitar diagonally in the other. Bistro tables on the sidewalk in orange and yellow and a mutt the color of charcoal sitting in the open doorway.

She parked along the street and stuck the envelope under the seat. Locked the doors. She stared at the café and said well hell's bells they do have some color in this godforsaken place. A woman hiding behind the newspaper at one of the bistro tables was the only other customer.

Annette walked inside. Muddy Waters from the speakers and a glass case filled with muffins and biscuits and sandwiches wrapped tightly in clear wrap. A note stuck on front of the case announced BEIGNETS, WE GOT EM. A little man shot up from behind the counter with a sharp hey and Annette jumped and slapped her hand across her heart.

'Sorry,' he said. 'Got a quarter rolled away from me and I can't find the damn thing nowhere.' His cheeks were pink and soft wrinkles crossed his forehead. He wore a tie-dye shirt and a button pinned to the collar asked you to smile.

'Only coffee,' she said.

'Those biscuits just came out,' he said.

'I already ate.'

'I can wrap one up for you. Eats good all day.'

Behind her the El Camino stopped at the corner. Paused and then crossed the street and parked in a nearly empty lot on the other side of a van.

'Fine,' she said.

He winked. Shifted his shoulders in rhythm with the music as he wrapped a biscuit in white paper and then poured her coffee. When he slid the bag and cup across the counter he said you should charge admission for all there is to see on you.

'I do,' she said and she took the bag and coffee and went out to the sidewalk. She sat down where the woman with the newspaper had been. The paper left behind on the bright yellow tabletop. She held it up and scanned the front page. Then searched each headline inside and on the back page. No mention of a fatal accident. No mention of a missing sum of money. She folded the paper and set it on the table and lifted her eyes into the clouds.

She was convinced that in each of her great moments of transition she had been delivered to decision by some silent whisper from a God who could not help but give a damn. The chance of getting ahold of the heart of a tattoo artist who would feed her habit. This body that was curved and firm in all the right places by no effort of her own. The strip club billboards that seemed to appear every half mile the day she packed her car and left the tattoo artist, the billboards that called to her and said this is what you are looking for. The butterfly on her wrist that flashed in the stage spotlight two years later and told her your time in the Stallion is done. A warm spring evening only a couple of weeks after she had walked out of the Stallion, before there had even been time for her image to be removed from those billboards, when driving again with her eyes open for what might be next she saw the carnival lights against the coming dusk and again her answer had been delivered. She replayed each moment in her mind and the simplicity with which each decision seemed to have been delivered. A guiding hand that reached out and motioned her to come this way. And she did not argue or second guess but only accepted the answer and then placed her own fingers between the guiding fingers and let herself be pulled into the new world waiting for her.

She stared blankly out toward the broken clouds and the patches of blue in between. The mutt moved from the doorway and came and lay down by her feet. She unwrapped the biscuit and broke it into two pieces and set one piece at the mouth of the dog. It lifted its head from the sidewalk and sniffed the biscuit and then licked at it. And then she crossed her legs. Folded her hands on top of her knee. And in this moment of thoughtfulness she decided this money and its deliverance was the voice of her Lord.

But this time was different because of Baron. She had seen what he was capable of when one of the workers argued about how much he was getting paid and called him a cheap ass or if a fight broke out at the carnival between roughnecks who had drunk a few too many beers in the parking lot. Violent and strong and adept at hurting someone. But he had only shown tenderness to her. A calm between them from the beginning. A calm that had grown with time as they spent nights sitting in lawn chairs and sipping beers once the carnival lights and bells and whistles had disappeared until tomorrow. Sometimes lamenting and sometimes reveling in this life they shared. A life of movement and sometimes danger and sometimes serenity. Baron telling her of his upbringing on the farm in the Arkansas lowlands. Three brothers and two sisters. A momma who never once looked anything but worn slap out. A daddy who repeated the same five or six sentences over and over. Fists in the kitchen on a sweltering starlit night in the middle of a drought and then Baron's feet on the dusty road and the stars that carried him away from there, never to see that place again. Never a letter or a phone call and wondering when his mother had died and wondering when his father had died and wondering if his brothers and sisters still had their feet in that familiar dirt or if they too had struck out with the same intensity and chalky taste of scorn in their mouths.

And then his years in and out of jailhouses. Stealing and drinking and pushing and shoving. A young man getting old quick. I just decided I was done with it, he had told her. Just like that. So I got whatever job I could get and I didn't never spend a nickel more than what would keep me alive. Slept in YMCAs and halfway houses. Kept that money in my pocket and I did whatever I could to keep some there. Worked on road crews and loaded freight on the docks. Washed dishes and worked on a damn garbage truck. Didn't make no difference to me. And I looked up one day and I'll be a son of a bitch if I didn't have a little stash and I sure enough emptied it out on this shit show you see now. Bought it with straight up cash money from some old guy who said he'd had enough. He was going home. I didn't have no home so I gave him half of what he wanted and he tried to tell me how to make it all official but all I said was give me the damn keys. He said what keys and I told him to just go on. It's mine now. Damn near twenty years ago but it don't feel like it. I've grown old.

You're not old she would tell him and pat his arm. Just mean. She would smile and hand him another beer from the cooler between their chairs. She would catch him looking at the stars and had many times imagined him walking down that Arkansas road with nothing but the determination he carried. He had talked to her and she liked listening and she had begun to feel something for Baron. Something fatherly or at least like she had always imagined a father to be.

She reached down and scratched the dog behind its limp ear. Sipped the coffee and looked along the empty sidewalk.

The only thing she knew about her own father was that he was a fighter. It was the only sentence her mother had ever used in the handful of times she had mentioned him. Some kind of fighter I met in a bar somewhere in Mississippi. Or maybe it was Louisiana. No it was Mississippi over on the river side. Around Greenville or Greenwood or one of them wore out Delta towns. He was a hard man. I remember that. Not hard like mean but his shoulders and back were like concrete. Spent two nights with him and he wanted me to come watch him fight but I couldn't handle that. Nine months later and there you were. Said with such a layer of indifference that Annette had grown up asking for this story over and over again, hoping to hear it told in some other way. Maybe with affection or a dash of the sentimental or maybe with the suggestion of gratitude. It was a come-and-go in some forgetful place but look at what it gave me. It gave me you. But instead her mother only repeated the same handful of sentences with the flat unchanged delivery. Did you ever tell him about me, Annette asked once. Ten years old and curious and finally brave enough to say it out loud. Why should I and God knows where the hell he is anyhow. I might could dig up his name if I thought real hard. It was a short name. At least his first name was. Seems like his last name had a little music in it. Or something different from what you're used to hearing and he kept telling me it meant something. Like that mattered. He was hard as nails but I could tell in the two days I was with him, there were pieces missing inside. Almost like he was waiting for something that was never gonna happen. But don't ask me nothing like that again, Annette. You'll understand this shit one day. She had done what her mother said and never asked again and then the debate began in her young mind – am I a beautiful thing on this earth or was I never meant to be at all?

She uncrossed her legs. Traced her finger along the outline of a hawk-wing on the outside of her thigh. And then for the rest of the morning she sat at the bistro table and barely moved as if posing for a sculptor. Turned her head only slightly when a car passed or the mutt moved from her to another customer who had more to offer. A pensive expression on her face and twice the little man in the tie-dye asked if she needed anything and twice she shook her head ever so slightly as if her neck had tightened and he believed he was being mocked in some sarcastic way that he didn't understand. By the time the early lunch customers began to trickle in, she had decided.

Here I am again, she thought. And a dash of adrenaline flowed through her. Standing at the edge and looking out into nothing and a wind at her back that promised to carry her.

She wanted to fly quickly before she changed her mind. In the night she had promised to wait on the money to reveal its answer to her but now she felt unsettled. Unsure. Nervous about this place. She stood from the bistro chair and walked to her truck and opened the door. Felt under the seat to make sure the money was still there though the vehicle was only steps away from where she had been sitting. She adjusted the rearview mirror. Opened and closed the glove compartment. Made a quick inventory of what she needed from the camper but she could only think of things that could be replaced. Clothes and shoes and a toothbrush and magazines and a hairdryer. Nothing that an envelope of money could not supply and in her mind the blood was wiped from it and it was now the vessel into her next life. She had swapped her old Toyota for the truck when she began with the carnival and it belonged to her. She closed her eyes and mentally scanned the camper once more for necessity or anything that might hurt her if left behind. A credit card or important piece of mail or photograph but there was nothing.

Nothing, she said aloud. I have nothing.

No, she answered. You said it wrong. You have no one.

And then she realized it was not uncertainty that she felt and recognized. It was loneliness. You have no one here or there or anywhere.

But you also have no one to slow you down. She rolled down the window and cranked the truck and she thought again of Baron. For the sake of her conscience and to appease the guilt of disappearing from the lawn chair he would set out for her, she wanted to leave half the money with him. But she believed that seeing him would change her mind and by dark she would be on the stage again, waiting for strangers to pay the fee to leer and suggest. She knew she had a narrow window of time to slip in and out, as he would be busy getting the carnival up and running though he was a watchdog with the crew. Little came and went that he did not notice. Go fill up the truck with gas, she thought. And then go by the carnival. Hide half the money in the Suburban. Write a note and leave it on the dashboard and then drive and wherever you end up tonight, maybe you will be able to sleep. She nodded at herself in the rearview mirror and then she shifted into drive and drove fast through the empty streets, feeling the surge of a new beginning. But not driving too fast for the El Camino to keep up.

18

JACK EMERGED FROM THE MOTEL ROOM on Friday morning and into the light of day like a vision of the weak and the damned. A forearm held across his brow. Limping from a tight lower back. Bloodred eyes and parched lips. He drew his shoulders up and grimaced. Opened his fingers and grabbed at the crown of his head and the pain twisted down his spine. He held his breath and waited for it to recede and then he returned inside. He moved to the sink and drank two cups of water. Then he picked up the bag of pills Big Momma had given him. Only four remained. Three red and one blue.

He set the bag down. Across the room the clock on the nightstand read 10:09 a.m. Ten hours from nightfall and that was when she would want the fight to begin. Ten hours to figure a way out.

What he had found in the lost hours in the motel room was fear. No matter how much he drank or how many pills he took, he could not chase away the idea that he would die in the cage if he had to fight. He feared taking any more blows to the head. He feared how slow his reactions would be if he drugged himself enough to tolerate the blows to the head. He feared where his mind might be if he did make it through the fight and woke up the next morning. Would he even know himself? Big Momma Sweet had not mentioned fixing the fight and this meant she would have someone in the cage with him who would push him to the absolute limits. An opponent who would try to break him. Scar him. Ruin him. Like she wanted to do to him. He had found fear and it had settled beside his every thought and situated itself next to the place inside that wanted to be beside Maryann. The house was gone. There was no way around that. He didn't have twelve thousand dollars to give Big Momma Sweet and he wasn't going to have thirty thousand dollars to keep the house from going to sale in five more days. Fear had grabbed him and fear wanted him to live. But how?

He sat on the bed and turned the pages in the notebook until he found the map he had drawn that would lead him to the shack on Maryann's land where he had taken all the furniture from the house. Furniture that he believed he could load up and then drive around Clarksdale to pawnshops and antiques stores and take what he could get. Maybe he could come up with two or three thousand. Maybe more. Maybe then he could take what he could get for the truck. Somehow scare up six or seven thousand dollars that he could take to Big Momma Sweet and use to ask for a reprieve. Or beg for a reprieve. Somehow buy himself a few more days because that's all he believed Maryann had left. And after he watched her close her eyes for the last time he would run like hell.

But the truck, he thought. Busted windshield and headlight. Dented and the engine hissing and smoking and God knows what else there is. All the money he had left was wadded on the floor and he eased down from the bed and straightened the bills. He had four hundred dollars separate from the twelve thousand when he left the casino. Now he was down to two hundred and five. He laid the bills in a stack and folded them.

Got to his feet and put on a shirt and went out to the truck.

The engine turned in a dry and grinding whine and smoke rose from the spaces around the hood. He quit trying to crank it and walked to the motel office. When he opened the door the woman behind the desk looked over the glasses on the end of her nose and asked if she needed to call a doctor.

'I don't need a doctor,' he said. 'I need a mechanic.'

Her hair was in big curls and held firmly in place by the power of hair spray and the smell made the sick man a little sicker.

'A mechanic,' he said again. 'And hurry up if you got an answer cause I'm about to vomit.'

'We warned you about puking on these premises. And you better quit running around naked.'

'Do you know a mechanic or not?'

'My brother. He ain't no genius, though.'

'Where is he?'

'Probably asleep. He likes to stay up all night.'

'That does not matter,' Jack said and he bent over and dryheaved.

'Lord Almighty,' the woman said. She stood and craned her neck over the top of the desk to see if anything was coming out.

Jack heaved and hacked and then set his elbow on the counter. Wiped at the sides of his mouth with his fingers, his face a bright red as if scorched.

'Where's your idiot brother?' he said.

'I didn't say he was an idiot. I said he ain't no genius.'

'Can he get here quick?'

'I reckon. He's right down there in number 11.'

'Then call him for me.'

She sat down and dialed her brother. When he answered she explained there was a man in the office who needed some help with his truck. Yeah, right now, she said and she hung up.

Jack sat on the tailgate and waited half an hour. Every passing minute an anxious fleck of time running out. He smoked a few cigarettes and drank some water and as the sun climbed higher in the late morning he began to sweat. A sour sweat, his body pushing out all the bad. When the door to number 11 opened Jack eased off the tailgate and popped the hood of the truck. A paunchy and paleskinned man crossed the parking lot and he propped one foot on the front fender while he looked over into the engine and didn't look at or speak to Jack. His hair was wet and unkempt and he wore a loosely tied bathrobe with no shirt underneath and sweatpants.

'I thought that woman in there said you were a mechanic.'

The man reached across the engine and tugged on a plug and pulled at a belt.

'It's the damn radiator,' Jack said. 'It's cracked and won't hold water.'

'Then what you need me for?'

'I need you to fix it.'

'Well. You're gonna need a new radiator.'

'No shit.'

'And I ain't got one.'

'If you did would you know what to do with it?'

'Yeah. Put it where that one right there is at.'

Jack spit and rubbed his face with his hands. He had taken one of the four remaining pills but it didn't keep his head from throbbing and he was hungry but too sick to eat and he needed the truck and he needed it right now.

'Where's the closest parts store?' he asked.

'About a mile that way,' the man said and he nodded north.

Jack then snatched one of his hands. The man said hey and tried to yank it free but Jack held it. Looked at the soft white fingers and clean fingernails and then he let it go.

'If you get my engine tore down and can't get it put together I'm gonna do something you ain't gonna like. It's got to be done right and it's got to be done fast as you can do it.'

The man drew back his hand. Looked Jack up and down. 'You don't look like much to me,' he said. 'But if it'll make you feel any better, I'll get it done and I'll get to it right now if you got some money.'

'I got some money.'

'Good then,' he said. 'Now all you need is a radiator.'

By God's own wonder we got one, the man said at the parts store when he slid the radiator to Jack across the counter. It was used but it would hold water and Jack tucked it under his arm and hurried the mile back along the side of the highway to the motel. The radiator was a heavy rectangle and it kept slipping from his grasp until he finally held it with both hands and raised it over his head and began a wheezing jog. His arms tiring and stopping to lower them. Adjusting his grip. Then raising the radiator above his head again and going as fast as he could go. This staggered routine of hurry and recovery until he finally returned to find the motel mechanic standing over the engine with tools in his hands.

He handed off the radiator and left him to work. He sat in the motel room with the door open and watched a soap opera. Beautiful women and beautiful men living their tangled lives in beautiful homes. Shiny hair and flawless skin and sparkling tears on cheeks. When the beautiful people were done for the day he looked over the pages of his notebook. The jigsaw puzzle of his life. He came to the page with the drawing of Maryann's jewelry box and he took a pen from the bedside table. Underneath NO NO NO and the trace of dates when he had held the box in his hands he wrote *This is all that is left.* And he felt a small relief in knowing the furniture would keep him from her precious things.

But the red digits of the clock on the nightstand kept changing. He stood in the doorway and walked up and down the row of motel rooms and nothing made the man work as fast as Jack needed him to work. I need to eat, he thought. I need to be rolling the second he's done. I need the strength it will take to get the furniture loaded out of the shack and into the back of the truck without another set of hands to help.

He went to the sink and stuck the pill bag in his pocket. Grabbed the foreclosure notice and folded it and then he picked up the dusty hardcover Bible and tucked the notice inside. He took the Bible and the notebook and he went out and set it all on the seat of the truck. He asked the motel mechanic how much longer and from beneath the engine the mechanic began to hum as if the noise would aid his calculation. The man had taken off his cheap digital watch and it set on the car battery. Jack snatched it and didn't wait for the answer and then he walked across the parking lot to the motel office. He paid what he owed and turned in the room key and then he took another walk alongside the highway. He had passed a Shell station on his walk back and forth between the parts store and the motel and the sign out front promised the coldest beer and cheapest tobacco in town.

It was almost one o'clock when he sat down on the curb outside the store with a Coke and chicken-on-a-stick and a pack of woodtip cigars and a bottle of Tylenol. Fucking hurry up, he thought. Imagining the mechanic asleep beneath the engine. Imagining Big Momma Sweet sharpening her knives. Imagining Ern twirling the branding iron like a baton. He took small bites of the chicken. Swallowed five of the Tylenol, trying to save the pills for later. He then stuck a woodtip cigar between his teeth just as a pickup pulled into the lot and stopped at a gas pump.

He watched as the woman got out. The high shorts and the tattoos. Dark hair trailing down around her shoulders and the sleeves of her t-shirt rolled up. She was unfazed by a truckload of working men who began to applaud as she pumped her gas. Unfazed as a teenage boy filling the tank of his mother's car stared until his mother called out for him to pay attention to what he was doing. And then an El Camino turned in and parked next to her truck. A slickfaced man got out and said something Jack couldn't hear but then he heard it when she said get the hell away from me.

The man shuffled closer to her. She finished with the gas and returned the nozzle to its cradle. More words between them. Less space between them. She moved away from him and he grabbed her by the back of her shirt. Jack stepped from the curb and was walking toward them when the woman wheeled around and caught the man with the whip of a backhand. He retreated a step. Opened his mouth and stretched his jaw. He lurched to grab her again but it was Jack who caught him this time. Snatching his wrist and twisting his arm behind his back. Jack shoved him onto the hood of the El Camino as he yelled turn loose of my damn arm.

'You better settle down,' Jack said.

'Go ahead and break it,' the woman said.

'Let me go, asshole.'

'Not until you get still,' Jack said.

'Who the hell are you anyway?'

'The man who's gonna break your arm,' the woman said.

The man kicked back at Jack and caught him in the knee. Jack gritted his teeth and twisted his arm higher and said she's right if you do that shit one more time.

'I just got to talk to her,' he said and he gave up. No more squirming and no more kicking. Jack eased the tension on the man's arm and asked her if it was okay to let him go.

'He doesn't scare me,' she answered. 'But me and him got nothing to talk about.'

'The hell we don't,' he said.

'I'm gonna let you go,' Jack said. 'But you get up easy.'

Jack released his arm. The man lifted himself from the hood of the El Camino. Rubbed at his shoulder. Then he told her again. We got to talk and I don't care if Captain America does stand here and listen. You're gonna tell me about you and Baron and what happened the other night. Or else.

19

THE DOOR OF THE CONVENIENCE STORE opened and a stumpy woman in camouflage pants and a camouflage t-shirt came toward them in a wobbly walk, calling for them to break it up right now or I'll call the law.

'You don't need to do that,' Ricky Joe said.

'I guess you would say that seeing as how you're the one who started it.'

'We don't need the law,' Annette said.

'You sure?'

Jack stepped back from them and then the woman looked at him and said hold on a second.

'What?'

She eased closer to him. Then began to shake her head.

'Son of a gun,' she said. 'It *is* you. Jack Boucher. I'll be damned. The Butcher standing right here in front of me after all these years. You know who I am?'

'I don't seem to recall.'

'Andy Clark's sister. You and him used to fight the same nights up in Memphis. We were all a lot younger then. You ain't still fighting?'

Annette had been keeping her eyes on Ricky Joe but when

the woman mentioned fighting, she turned her attention to Jack.

'Do I look like I could win a fight?'

'What you look like never seemed to matter. I watched you enough to know only God above has you figured out.'

'I wouldn't go that far,' he said.

'What the hell are you doing in Clarksdale?'

'I'm in that motel right up the road.'

'What for? What about that big old house? You still got it?'

'For now.'

The woman kept talking to Jack about her brother and some night somewhere when something happened and Annette studied him while she went on. His knobby knuckles. His scarred forehead. The way his mouth and neck shifted when he spoke as if it might hurt. While the woman talked and Annette watched, Ricky Joe was moving around to the driver's side door of Annette's truck. He eased up on the handle and inched it open and was about to slide in and look around when Jack pointed.

Annette came toward Ricky Joe but she was beaten to him by the woman in camouflage who stomped over and shook her finger in his face and told him he better get out of here right now or the next person he'd be talking to would be wearing a badge. Ricky Joe moved from Annette's truck, his hands held up and backing away from the woman as if she might sink her teeth into his flesh.

When the woman was done scolding she turned back to Jack and slung her arms around his waist and hugged. He grunted and hugged her back and then she said I can't believe I didn't figure you out when you came in the store. I guess you look better from far off.

'We all do,' he said. 'But for now I have to go.' He walked over to the curb and picked up the cigars and Tylenol and headed back toward the motel.

The woman turned again to Ricky Joe and Annette. 'You better go settle this somewhere else,' she said and then she went back inside the store.

'I'm calling Baron,' Annette said.

'Good,' Ricky Joe answered. 'Call him. And you can tell him what I'm telling you. I saw you and him out there at the wreck. I saw him pick up something and I saw you both study it and hide it away and I want to know what it is. Because I saw something else out there too. I saw someone lying on the ground. Maybe it was somebody breathing. Maybe it wasn't. But whatever it was he told us to drive off and we left that person out there in the dark. You and him think didn't nobody see. But I did.'

'You didn't see nothing cause there wasn't nothing to see.'

'You got a little secret. That's okay. We all got those. I'm just interested in what it is. If you're not willing to share then I'm guessing the local sheriff might listen to what I got to say.'

'Go ahead. I'll drive you there. They'd probably lock you up for about a dozen other things before you could get your mouth open.'

'Come on then.'

'I'm not going anywhere with you.'

'That's fine,' he said. And then he pulled a knife from his pocket. Snapped it open and stabbed the front tire of her truck. There was a pow and a hiss and he said you ain't going nowhere at all. And you remember what I said I'll do.

He climbed into the El Camino and shifted into drive and then he was gone, a blue cloud of exhaust trailing behind. The woman came back out of the store and stood next to Annette and said I saw it all. I'll call the police now.

'Don't,' Annette said. 'He's gone.'

'You got somebody who can come help you?'
'Yeah. I just need to use the phone.'

Annette followed the woman inside the store and around behind the counter. She waited in the open door of the office while the woman wrote down the store address on a slip of paper. Then she handed the address and cordless telephone to Annette.

She dialed Baron and told him about Ricky Joe. About him sticking the knife in the tire and she asked for him to come to the Shell station. No, don't send somebody else and no I don't need help changing it. Get over here because we got to talk. And hurry up. She gave him the address and said I'll be waiting with the truck. She set the phone on the desk and then returned to the counter and asked the woman for a pack of Marlboros.

'Let me ask you something,' Annette said. 'That man out there before. How long have you known him?'

'I suppose twenty-some-odd years.'

'And he's a fighter?'

'Was.'

'What kind?'

'The good kind,' she said. 'At least when he started out.'

'No. I mean like boxing or what?'

'Boxing? Shit. He's a fighter of the first kind. Nothing but air between fists and faces.'

'What'd you call him? The butcher?'

'That's right.'

'Why?'

'Boucher is his last name. You gotta say it just right. Boo-shay. That means butcher in French. He'd sure as hell carve you up with those hands.'

'Jack Boucher,' Annette said. 'He's from around here?'

'Yeah. But I don't think he's lived here for a while. At least I don't never see him no more.'

'How far away is that motel he said he was staying at?'

'About a quarter mile. Why? You think you know him?'

'Nah. Just curious.'

'He's a damn good man to get curious about. He's been rode hard and put up wet but I guarantee you he's got some stories to tell.'

'How old is she?'

She shrugged. 'At least as old as me and I'm about to be forty-six come September.'

Annette went outside to the truck to wait on Baron, but she thought about Jack Boucher. A fighter. Easily old enough to be a father to a woman of twenty three. She opened the glovebox and took out a map she used to mark the towns the carnival had visited to help Baron avoid repeats. I was with him around Greenville or Greenwood or one of them wornout Delta towns, her mother had said. And he bragged his name meant something. She didn't remember what. Annette moved her finger across the flatland of northwest Mississippi and found Clarksdale. Near the river. Close to the names of the towns her mother had mentioned and what she had seen so far of this place sure as hell fell into the category of wore out. She wished now she would have touched his back or shoulders to feel if they were hard like concrete, the only physical detail her mother had ever given about the man Annette had always wondered about.

Boucher means butcher, the woman in camouflage had said.

A name that meant something. The scratch of information from her mother less of a throwaway and more of a prospect now that there was a real man she could attach it to.

She set the map aside and got out of the truck. Walked out

to the road and looked in the direction he walked. And in the distance she saw the motel sign.

She was a dozen steps along the roadside when Baron arrived and parked next to her. She returned to the gas pump and stood with him at the deflated tire and when he asked where she was going she only shrugged.

'What is Ricky Joe's problem?' Baron asked.

'I don't know but you need to listen. He knows about the body we left out there. I guess he got out and spied on us the other night at the wreck because he saw it all. You kneeling over it and then us finding the envelope. He doesn't know if the person was dead or alive or what exactly we found but just that we found something and he wants to know.'

'What'd you tell him?'

'I didn't tell him anything. But he's acting crazy and he threatened to call the sheriff and tell about the body if we don't let him in on whatever we found.'

'Damn it,' Baron said.

'I know,' she answered. 'I don't like this place. We got off to a bad start and we should've just kept going. A dead man and us holding on to this money and now Ricky Joe wanting a cut of whatever is floating around in his mind. But that's not even the problem. The problem is him shooting off his damn mouth or at least threatening us with it until kingdom come. You don't need that noose around your neck. You know what bad luck is as well as I do.'

Baron crossed his arms. Stared at the tire and huffed. 'You sound like you think he's serious.'

'Serious enough to chase me down. Serious enough to pull a damn knife out and stick it in my tire. Serious enough to make me think he might just do what he says. And you don't need that shit, Baron. If he does call the sheriff you'll be easy to find sitting out there in that parking lot. You and the rest of the convicts.'

'I'm not a convict. Not yet. And I don't plan on starting.'

He stepped past her and leaned the bench seat of her truck forward. Took out the lug wrench and the jack and set them on the ground next to the flat tire and then he moved around to the truck bed. Knelt down and reached under and turned the lever to release the spare.

'I know you said you don't need help changing the tire but let me do it anyhow,' he said. 'Working helps me think.'

She nodded and stood back. Watched him crank the jack. Loosen the lug nuts. I won't leave him now, she thought. Not tonight. Not until the show is on the road.

Changing the tire was an easy task for a man who had worked with engines and cars and carnivals and in only a few minutes Baron was done. They smoked a cigarette and Annette was about to ask him what he had decided when the woman stuck her head out of the store and asked them to get moving. You been blocking those pumps long enough today. And then she called out to Annette and said if you're still wondering about Jack Boucher I wouldn't go down to the motel.

'Why not?' Annette asked.

'Because there he goes,' she said and she pointed toward the road.

Baron and Annette turned to see a dented gray truck and Jack behind the wheel, his arm propped in the open window. The splintered windshield. The bent tailgate. A dull gray Chevy like the one Baron had once owned.

'Holy shit,' Baron said. 'That's the truck. That's the gray damn truck.'

'And I was just talking to the guy driving it.'

'Talking to him where?'

'Right here. Right before Ricky Joe stabbed the tire.'

'Are you sure?'

'Hell yeah I'm sure.'

'Holy shit,' Baron said again and he tossed the cigarette. 'We got dead bodies and found money and now this. I'm not waiting to let it pile up any higher. If we hustle we can be gone by midnight.'

He climbed in the Suburban and she climbed in the truck. He pulled out before her and turned to the left, in the direction of the carnival. But she stopped before following him onto the road. She looked to the right and the busted pickup was being driven by a man called Jack Boucher and the truck had paused to wait its turn at a four-way stop. Be ready for it when it comes, she remembered promising herself as she danced through the rain. And the urgency of Baron's voice and the sounds of the world around her faded into the background as she could hear the choir singing. She could hear the scripture being read. She could feel the pulse of the congregation and the strength of the holy church of coincidence that seemed to be once again delivering its message to her in a moment of need. To the left Baron sped away. To the right was a fighter whose name meant butcher and she knew she would never again be at peace with herself if she didn't follow him. There were a thousand things to consider now. Baron putting his hands on a dying man and a son of a bitch like Ricky Joe who had seen it all and now the truck reappearing and she knew that the envelope belonged somewhere in the middle of it all. She allowed several cars to pass going in Baron's direction while she watched Jack move up to the stop sign and then go on through. Several cars that put space and obstruction between her and Baron and he wouldn't know she wasn't following until too late. All the questions bounced around in her mind but there was only one she truly wanted to answer.

Could that be my father?

20

O N WEEKENDS THEY LOADED A PALE yellow Volkswagen van
with Maryann's creations and a table and two chairs and
a tent and they drove to places like Winona and Yazoo City and
Indianola and Grenada. Towns with arts or music festivals and
they popped the tent and set up the table and some makeshift
shelves and then the crowds came and moved along the streets,
carrying snow cones and corndogs and holding the hands of
children and they browsed what the artisans had to offer. She
talked while they sat under the tent. Told him she was an only
child and I know it gets boring out there sometimes but you
can find stuff to do. She told him her parents had died and she
was all that was left of a family that had been on that spot for
four generations. The house built in 1840 by her great great
grandfather. Some of those photos on the wall damn near as
old as the house. The land accumulated here and there over the
years until it topped out at two hundred acres. A measurement
of space he could not comprehend.

When there was music he would go and sit on the ground
near the flatbed trailer that served as a stage and watch as
the bands sweated and roared. He liked the bluesmen who
seemingly could not play a note or sing a word without some

contortion of the face and body and it was in those moments of lyrical anguish that the boy felt his blood rush, weaving through his body with the grind of the guitar and the call of the harmonica and he listened hypnotically and often his own face would mimic that of the bluesmen and shift in impulsive spasms. When the festival was done for the day they would break down the tent and load up the shelves and ceramics and he would hold his head out of the window as they drove the highway, the summer sun low in the sky and Maryann humming along with the radio and the peaceful land and sky of home waiting for them.

When he was seventeen years old he saw a flyer tacked to a light pole on a street corner in Water Valley. A Saturday of selling ceramics over and he had helped Maryann load the Volkswagen van and gone in search of a bathroom. Shops were closed along Main Street and he ducked into an alley and pissed behind a garbage can. Walking out of the alley he saw the flyer that read FIGHTERS WANTED.

He snatched it from the pole. The flyer had been written in sloppy script and photocopied and it advertised a local fighting event for the coming weekend and the event needed bodies. Anyone eighteen years old and willing was eligible. Three rounds. Bare knuckles. Cash prizes to the winners. He folded the flyer and stuck it in his pocket and returned to the van and as he and Maryann drove back to Clarksdale he was already figuring out a plan to get to the event.

The next Saturday he told her he had been invited to a party. She asked him what party and where it was and who was throwing it and he had all the madeup answers ready. He knew she would not argue because she would be both happy and surprised that he had such an invitation and then when

Saturday arrived he drove off in the late afternoon as she sipped a beer on the front porch.

It took a little more than an hour to drive to Water Valley. He stopped at a gas station and asked directions to the local VFW and then he went into the bathroom and changed from the new button-down collar shirt Maryann had bought him for the party into a dingy t-shirt he wore working with her in the potter's barn. He wet a comb under the faucet and slicked his hair back, believing this made him appear older. And then he found his way to the VFW.

It was a brick building with white, scarred doors in the front. He was an hour and a half ahead of when the event was scheduled to begin and only two cars were in the parking lot. He went in the doors into a large open room. Foldout chairs were pushed against the walls and three old men worked to erect a stage made from plywood and two-by-fours. In the corner of the room were a roll of chicken wire and several metal poles.

Jack walked over to the men. They paused, looked up with red faces. Then they turned back to the job.

'I'm here to fight,' Jack said.

'Set this son of a bitch down,' one of the men said. They propped the corner of the stage on a short stack of cinderblocks and the three men raised up groaning and grabbing at their forearms or shoulders.

The man who spoke eyed Jack. Pulled a handkerchief from his back pocket and wiped his forehead. A long ash hung from the cigarette dangling at the corner of his mouth and the ash crumbled and fell like a tiny snowfall. 'You ain't old enough,' he said.

Jack removed the flyer from his pocket. Unfolded it and showed it to the man.

'I know what that is,' the man said. 'I made it.'

'Says right there you don't have to be but eighteen,' Jack said and he tapped his finger on the number as if to clarify.

The man cleared his throat. Tossed his cigarette onto the concrete floor. 'Only problem being you're no such thing.'

'Hell I ain't,' Jack said.

'What you think, boys?' the man said to the others. 'He look eighteen to you?'

'It all depends,' one of them said.

'On what?'

'On whether or not he's got the entry fee.'

The man pulled a pack of cigarettes from his shirt pocket and shook one free. 'Well,' he said. 'You heard him. You eighteen or not?'

Jack had the cash, his part from what Maryann gave him for his help each weekend. He held out a twenty and the man took it. He sized Jack up again and said you're littler than most anybody we got. You sure about this?

'You just tell me when and where,' Jack said and he poked out his chest and cocked his pointed shoulders.

The men laughed and then focused again on raising what would become the floor of the makeshift fighting cage. Then the man with the cigarette said you'll go first and get it over with. Bring a mouthpiece. I know it says bare knuckles but you need some athletic tape to wrap your fists. No crotch or eye shit. Three rounds. Two minutes each. And we can call it any second or if you holler quit it's over.

'I won't be hollering quit,' he said.

'You don't know what you might do. Be here and ready at the start time. God knows I don't want you to miss your bedtime and have your momma come looking for us.'

Ninety minutes later he fought a man who had five years, thirty pounds, and four inches on him. He fought a man he could not reach and he could not lift and he could not get away from. The sparse crowd sat close to the chicken wire cage and drank from pints of rye or gin. Hollered for him to keep running and maybe try to dig a hole to crawl into or if you got a gun stuck in them britches it might be a good time to snatch it out and make use of it.

Jack was strong but lean and his lanky arms and legs were easy to get hold of by the taller and stronger man and just when he was on the edge of crying mercy from an arm lock or leg bend, Jack would twist his slippery body and slide free. Just when a hard right and then another hard right landed he somehow managed to straighten his legs and get upright and wave the man across the plywood floor to come on. We ain't done. The howls from the crowd growing louder but beginning to turn his way. The mockery gone from the voices and replaced with cries of encouragement. Cries of motivation. As he stood with his fists up, calling for the opponent to get back over here, he glanced out at the crowd. Surprised they were on his side and he began to feel something more than the need for surviving this fight. He felt the need to win it. The boy busted and swollen and the cigarette smoke like a staggered veil across the fluorescent lights and he heard his name being called. Come on, Jack. Don't give up, Jack. Hit him, Jack. And the stronger man heard it too and the frustration of not being able to make the boy quit multiplied as the voices urged the boy to fight on and he charged Jack in what he thought to be a flurry of victory, but he was instead met with a quick slip and a straight hard fist that connected in an unexpected jolt between the nostril and cheekbone. A fist that put the man to sleep and the next time he opened his eyes a stick of smelling salt was crammed against his nostril and the boy was long gone down the highway with the windows rolled down and the music loud and a cash prize of fifty dollars stuffed into his sweaty shoe.

There was no way to hide from Maryann when he returned from Water Valley. He walked through the kitchen door and found her sitting at the table. She looked up at him and when she saw his battered face she dropped the magazine she had been reading.

'I'm okay,' he said.

And she started right up like he expected. What happened and where have you been? Who did this to you and what about the party and don't you lie to me like that. How did they let you fight when you're barely old enough to drive and I'm going to call the police in Water Valley right now and let me get you some ice though you don't deserve it after pulling a prank like this.

'I'm sorry,' he said after he had answered all the questions. 'I didn't want to lie but I knew you wouldn't let me go. I just wanted to see what it was like.'

'See what it was like?'

'Yeah. The fight.'

'You know what a fight is like. You've been in too many.'

'This is different. It's a real ring and a referee sits there and stops it if it goes bad.'

'Did he forget? Because it looks like it went bad.'

'Not as bad as it did for the other guy. I won. And they cheered me.'

'Who cheered? People watch this?'

'Some.'

'This is bullshit, Jack. You look like you've been in a car wreck.'

'I know. I'm sorry.'

'Stop saying that because you're not.'

'I am about the lying part. I only wanted to see what it was like.'

He sat down at the table and held his head back as she examined the places where the fists and elbows had landed. One bloodshot eye and crusted blood in a nostril and a fingernail scratch running across the side of his neck. A swollen upper lip and bulbous cheeks. She shook her head as she studied his face and he said ouch as she touched a fingertip to tender spots. She filled a Ziploc bag with ice cubes and gave him a glass of water and a few aspirin. She poured herself a short glass of bourbon and they sat together at the table. He then reached down and pulled the fifty dollars from his sock. Unfolded the bills and laid them on the table and he looked at the prize in admiration.

'My first winnings,' he said.

'And your last,' she answered. He nodded and apologized again and she stared at him and didn't know what to say. She only knew this was a beginning, a step toward something she could not understand.

After he won his first fight the changes came. Coming home after school and setting his books and workout bag on the kitchen table. Already sweating from using the weight room at the high school. Saying hey to Maryann if he saw her and if he didn't see her he yelled it out and hoped his voice would find her. And then he would walk out of the house and to the road and run. He jogged along the straightline highway, waving at passing work trucks and watching the crop dusters rise and fall, leaving cloudy trails of insecticide across the valuable land. He did not wear a watch or mark his distance. He only ran until he felt like he had pushed himself far enough from the house to make it a struggle to get back and on the days when his young body felt the urge to go and go and go he would not return until the sun was beginning to set and burn across a fiery horizon.

Sometimes Maryann would stand in the yard and watch him run until he was out of sight. Other times she would sit at the kitchen table and see what books he had brought home as he had recently discovered the library. He read about military history. About war and the strategies that had won or lost. He read about the martial arts and their philosophies and he read about the most effective ways to bend or break another man. He read the biographies of great warriors who had become leaders of men and of driven athletes who had come from nowhere and ended up somewhere. And he read the ancient tales of conquest, where mortals overcame the challenges of giants and demons to win the favor of the gods. He tore his favorite pages from the books and taped them on the inside of his closet door, which she discovered one day while hanging clean shirts. A single piece of tape at the top middle of each page and the corners curled and the pages waved in the movement of the opening door. On each page a single sentence underlined in red ink. Appear weak when you are strong, and strong when you are weak. A thousand battles, a thousand victories. You can only fight the way you practice. No man or woman born, coward or brave, can shun his destiny.

She tried to detour him. She drove him to community colleges and sat with academic advisors and tried to sell him on working toward a degree or learning a special skill. Do something that not many other people do, she would say and almost before the words left her mouth she could see the reply in his eyes. I already am. He would sit politely and listen and fill out the applications. He would listen to Maryann compliment the cafeteria and dorms and brick buildings. She suggested he might like to study history because of what he had been reading and she went on about what all he might do if he went all the way through a four-year school and got a degree and he always nodded.

She could see him getting stronger. Harder. Taller. And she noticed the flyers lying around his room that announced the fights. He had promised he wouldn't lie about his age anymore. And he hadn't fought since the night in Water Valley. But he had been going to watch. To study the differences between success and failure. Hurting or being hurt. To figure out where to hold his hands or how to protect when it wasn't going so well or how to duck and slide to keep your opponent off balance. He began to tape his fists before he went out to run. He brought home a mattress he found on the side of the road and tied it around a tree in the backyard. She worried as she listened to him grunting as he punched and kicked the mattress until he was lathered in sweat. She didn't say anything when he let his hair grow longer because someone told him about the strength of the locks of Samson. She didn't say anything to him about his eighteenth birthday approaching. Because she knew that was what he was waiting on. She wanted to make him promise not to fight. She wanted to make him promise he would not participate in a violent world. To become what he wanted to become. To try.

But she couldn't make herself go all the way in her opposition. She discouraged him with suggestions of how a body breaks down when punished. She offered to help with tuition and told him he could live with her for as long as he wanted. This is your house as much as mine. She agonized over if she should protect him or let him follow this thing. Let him chase it. Allow him to find comfort in who he was. Like she had never been able to do. Tied to a place through the string of generations but never sure of her own self. Never able to be what she wanted in the land she loved and never strong enough to break free and go and try somewhere else. Be with someone who loved her in a way she had not known. She watched him in the soft light of the late afternoons as he chopped firewood or threw punches at the mattress. Listened to him talk about the art of war or the journey of Odysseus. Noticed that the expression in his young face was more peaceful and he never mentioned classmates or friends or the lack of those things anymore. He was finding solace in what he was doing and what he wanted to attempt. He was finding himself. And she admired him. She admired his grit and determination and his hellbent motivation toward this dangerous thing because she had stepped around her dangerous thing. Abandoned herself to hide from others and now her youth was gone. Her chances had disappeared. And his chances were before him and with each step he ran and each punch he threw into the mattress she could see him believing in himself. At night she lay awake and worried about him. Feared for him. But she could not make herself forbid him. No matter from which direction it had arrived.

21

S MOKE CAME FROM THE ENGINE OF the truck and it had stalled out on him as he slowed on the highway to look for the turnoff, but cranked again. The dirt road was a quarter mile from the house. Jack drove between the endless rows of soybeans, following the map in the notebook that led to the antique furniture. A tire tool he dug out from behind the seat of the truck against his leg, the tool he would use to try and pry open a window or a corner of the tin roof. In a couple of hundred yards the road made a lazy curve to the right and past a ridge of hardwoods he came to a levee. The map read TURN LEFT AT THE LEVEE and he did, following a path now instead of a road, the grass worn down where the drivers of large tractors with large tires drove underneath the shade of trees to eat lunch or steal short naps. He followed the path alongside the levee and then he saw the shack ahead. The leaning chimney and the walls fortified with ten-inch wide wooden planks. The shutters closed and nailed shut. He stopped and got out, leaving the engine running and hoping it wouldn't die. He walked around to the side of the shack and the ground was littered with beer bottles and an empty gas can and he knew already.

The chain and the combination lock that kept the front door

secured remained in place. But then he walked around to the back and scattered across the ground were more beer bottles and a left behind crowbar. Several of the wooden planks had been pried apart and a chainsaw had cut a rough rectangular hole in the back wall wide enough for the largest of the desks or armoires or handcrafted headboards to pass through. He leaned his head in. Stepped up and into the empty shack. Sawdust sprayed across the floor. The decaying corpse of a rat in the corner. THANKS spraypainted on the wall. A smiley face next to it.

Annette parked in the shade of a silo. She had lost him when he turned off on the dirt road, getting caught behind a lethargic eighteen-wheeler and by the time she was able to pass the busted truck was no longer on the highway. She knew it didn't have the get-up-and-go to speed away and she noticed the random dirt roads that split the acres and figured that was where he had gone. Except for a big white house with a little house behind it there was nothing but farmland in all directions. So she parked and waited.

It only took a few minutes for the truck to reappear. Smoking and rattling as it came past her. Moving slowly. She shifted into drive but paused when the truck turned into the gravel driveway at the great house. She watched it creep along and roll to a stop at the little house in the backyard. She wanted him to be alone when she approached him so she held for a moment, waiting to see if someone else may appear.

He opened the door to the potter's barn. A stranger staring at the past of another. One of the windows had blown open and a cluster of birds scattered when he pounded his foot. There was bird shit splattered on the floor and tables and he kicked over a stool as he made his way to the back corner where he had hung a punching bag years ago after Maryann could no longer work the wheel.

This is where you started, he thought. This is where you'll end.

He moved to the bag and went to work. Straight lefts and then straight rights. Then fists to the body and puffs of dust from the bag with each blow. The sweat coming on. Breathing hard so quickly but he did not stop. He shoved the bag and it swung at him and he dodged and countered. The skin of his knuckles breaking as he grunted and gasped and ignored the throbbing behind his eyes. He imagined his own face on the swinging bag and he tried to knock himself out and then he hugged the bag and bit at his own throat, the sweat and saliva blending with the dust as he pressed his face into the bag and when he couldn't get his teeth into it he stepped back and hit it with more quick jabs and a roundhouse right but he could not knock himself out and he punched and punched until he had no more and he dropped to a knee. Sweat dripped from the tip of his nose and his heartbeat hurried in quick, hard thumps. He grabbed at his chest and then he made a fist and punched himself in the forehead.

Get up. Fucking get up. You take a knee tonight and you're fucking dead. Get up because this is the last time you'll be in this place you never deserved anyway. All you did was prove them all right. You proved what a fucking problem you were and always have been and you proved that you'd ruin her if she signed it all over to you. All you did was everything everybody expected of you now get the fuck up. You won't ever surprise anyone and they're all laughing at you and nobody gives a shit about your headaches but you better not go down to a knee or whoever she has lined up for you will fucking beat you into the dirt and the crowd will cheer while your blood is being spilled. You better not fucking die before she does now get up. You can't get the fucking house back and you can't pay Big Momma and you'll never see Maryann again if you go down to a fucking knee. All you have left to give is your stupid fucking life for another day or week or however long she needs and you better not fucking die. Now get the fuck up.

He raised his head. In the corner he saw the iron poker he long ago used for the kiln and the kiln was what he had loved the most. Tall and rectangular and made of brick the color of sand. He would help Maryann build and stoke the fire and when the day disappeared he would stare at the burning orange of the inside of the kiln against the coming night and imagine it to be a fiery beacon. The last light of the world. He picked up the iron poker now and then he attacked the bag and his disgust was fueled when the bag would not split so he turned the weapon on everything else. The dustcovered pottery on the dustcovered shelves, small explosions of terracotta and clay as he attacked and screamed. And then the light bulb and the old porcelain sink and when he had busted all he could with the iron he then used his hands to overturn tables and throw stools and kick over the potter's wheel. Blood came from a cut on his hand and he was lathered in a polluted sweat and when he had nothing left to destroy he dropped to the floor. On his back and panting and he knew once he caught his breath and the adrenaline died away he would look around and have one more thing to regret. But he would not let some stranger have the things they had made together in the days of youth and trustfulness.

The punching bag still swung slightly. The room clouded with dust and debris. He pressed the cut on top of his hand against his jeans and as he held it there he noticed a widemouth vase in the corner. Unscarred. Hidden beneath one of the tables he had thrown aside. It sat uneven as if resting on a stone. He stood up and stepped across the damage and picked it up. Held it with both hands. Looked at the bottom at the cursive M she put on all her work. Touched his finger to the groove and ran it along the shape of the letter. He looked down where it had sat for so long and he noticed a latch attached to the floor plank where the vase had been.

He knelt and set the vase on the floor. He touched the latch but did not lift. Instead he sat down and wondered. Wondered if he had been the one to put it there. Wondered if beneath was something else he had hidden away. Maybe beneath was an answer. He touched the latch again. Imagined the other Jack having done this and there could only be bad news on the other side if that was who was responsible and this thought made him pull the latch and lift the plank.

A gray lockbox sat beneath the floor and he took it by the handle on the lid and raised it out and then he felt in the space beneath the floor for a key. There wasn't one. He tried to pry it open with his hands and when he couldn't he took the box and the vase and he left the potter's barn and returned to the kitchen.

He set the lockbox on the table and then he stood at the sink and washed the vase. The sole unbroken piece of what remained of her life's work. The filth in a brown swirl down the drain. Then he washed the cut on his hand. Grabbed a dishrag from a drawer and wrapped it around the cut. He looked at the wristwatch he had swiped from the mechanic and it was 3:41. I don't have time for this, he thought. Go see Maryann. But he believed the box had come from the other Jack and he couldn't make himself abandon it. He then took a knife and he sat down at the table with the box. He worked the knife between the lid and the box rim and pried it up until the lock popped and he folded the box open.

There were no notes from himself. No treasure or secret or promise from his past. Inside was a stack of envelopes and he lifted them out. A spider crawled out from the lockbox and he thumped it away and then he set the stack on the table. He picked up the first envelope and it was addressed to Maryann. And so was the next. All of them were addressed to Maryann and all of them came from someone with the initials JKM, which was the only inscription where the return address should have been. He counted and there were seventeen and they were stacked in what seemed to be chronological order. On some of the letters the postmark had faded away but on others he noticed the dates and the letters began in 1979 and stretched to June 1983. Most came from New Orleans but the last few arrived from Savannah.

He pushed his chair away from the table and tried to figure. I was twelve years old when I came to live here and that was in the summer of '82. So you were here when she hid these. When she decided they belonged in a lockbox underneath the floor. And this is something she doesn't want you to see. Something she doesn't want anyone to see.

But here it is.

Round Three

22

THERE WERE THINGS ABOUT HIS LIFE he could never know. What the people looked like who made him and what their names were and how he got his own name. If he had been held as a baby or left to himself and did he have a crib and was there a moment when he was loved. What was the weather like on the day he was born and did anyone help him learn to walk or did he just figure it out trying to either get to or away from something.

Secrets that existed through no fault of his own. He had not chosen to be born to those who did not care. He had not chosen to be a child dropped off at a secondhand store. He had not chosen the void. His secrets were simply a part of the world, withheld from him by a hand greater than his own.

He stared at the stack of letters and this was different. Maryann had kept this box under the floorboard in the potter's barn for a reason. This was her secret and she had made the decision to hide it away. He imagined her now at work at the wheel. Her wet hands molding the clay and her foot pressing the pedal that spun the stone wheel and her mind not on the creation in her fingertips but instead adrift with whatever dreams or heartbreak or ghosts she had hidden beneath the floorboard only steps away.

He wasn't sure if he should read them. Or if he wanted to. The letters were more than thirty years old. The last one written a year after he had come to live with her. It was her choice.

He stood up from the chair and moved to the sink. He lifted the vase and set it in the center of the small table. Took a glass from the cabinet and filled it with water.

Emptied his pockets. What was left of the cash and the brass knuckles. He took more Tylenol and looked at the three pills left in the bag, trying to save them until the fight was closer. He craned his neck. Raised his arms over his head and stretched, his body like some twisted cord that could not be undone.

He sat back down and opened the first letter. A smooth cursive hand, written in pencil. The script smudged and erased and rewritten in several places. The pages soft as if handled again and again. He read it and set it aside and opened the second letter. And then the third.

One after another and they all said the same things. Please come with me. Please. You and I both know we can't live the life we want to live in that little town. It's just not possible. You have to come with me. I know about your family and what they will think. I know what you feel about your responsibilities to all of it but we cannot live there. You know that. I just want us to be together.

As he went further through the stack the letters became more emphatic and the voice began to accuse. Maybe this is not what you want. Maybe you lied to me. Maybe none of it is real. He felt the hands reaching through the words and trying to grab hold of Maryann. Pull her forward. Dig her feet out of this black and fertile ground.

I will come get you. I don't want to think of you alone. I don't want to think of me alone. Please. Over and over the letters spoke of courage. Love. Beginnings. Endings. Regret. Being the way we are supposed to be.

He read until he reached the last letter. Its envelope did not hold multiple pages like the others but only a scrap of paper and he knew it to be some final declaration. A hard goodbye. He could tell by the way the note was ripped on the edge. It was a small scrap of paper resting there in its envelope but he felt its weight, so much heavier than all the others. So he did not take it out but instead closed the envelope and laid it on the pile.

In the quiet of the house he was struck by the revelation that she was more like him than he ever had imagined. She knew loneliness. Displacement. The feeling of living in a world you don't understand. And then he wondered what his role had been. Had he helped to keep her here? Had he given her an excuse to hide away? To be afraid. Did he get in the way?

Go and beg, he thought.

He pushed away from the table. Moved through the empty rooms of the house. Burn it all down, he thought. Just go ahead and burn it all down. He tried to see himself as a boy and tried to see Maryann but the house only felt like a coffin now. A holding for some unavoidable end. Take what is left. Burn it all down. And then go and beg Big Momma Sweet for your life so you can be sitting right next to her when she dies away from home. The place she gave everything to. Live through the night so you can be there and you can feel every grain of betrayal as you look at her lost and dying eyes and hide behind the curtain of what she doesn't know. Because you're nothing but a coward so go ahead and burn it all down. Do the last thing.

He passed through the hallway and returned to Maryann's bedroom. Opened the jewelry box. Removed his notes of warning and they floated to the floor in waves of resignation. Inside the box were pearl necklaces and diamond earrings and emerald rings. Gold bracelets and their gold charms. Lockets and necklaces adorned with rubies and petite diamonds that for a hundred years had been draped around smooth necks and dangled between pale breasts. He closed the lid and picked up the jewelry box and he crumpled his notes to himself and tossed them into the closet. He carried the box under his arm to the kitchen and set it on the table with the letters. He flexed his rigid fingers and then he dropped the last three pills into the Tylenol bottle and scooped the money and brass knuckles from the counter and stuffed it all back into his pockets. He set Maryann's letters inside the lockbox.

He checked the time on the watch. It was past four o'clock but that didn't seem to matter anymore. He removed the watch and set it on the table and then he walked over to the kitchen window and slammed his hand through the screen trying to kill the wasp, just as the truck pulled into the driveway.

23

JACK WALKED IN THE HIGH GRASS and when he came toward the truck she was standing there with her hands in the pockets of her cutoffs. He looked past her and across the road and then around the yard as if there might be others.

'What is it?' he said.

'You remember me?' Annette asked.

'You aren't easy to forget,' he said. 'Even for me.'

'What's that mean?'

'Nothing.'

She shifted her feet and took her hands from her pockets and pressed them together. 'Thanks again for helping out back at the store.'

'I didn't really do anything,' he said and he moved to his truck's door. 'Why was he messing with you anyway?'

'I don't know.'

Jack nodded and said I guess it's none of my business anyway. He opened the truck door and set the lockbox and the jewelry box on the seat next to the motel Bible and his notebook.

'What'd you do? Follow me?' he asked.

'Yeah.'

'What for? You a cop?'

'Do I look like a cop?' she said.

'Not one like I ever seen,' he said and he sat down behind the wheel.

'Then can I talk to you a second?' she said and she put her hand on the truck door. 'The woman at the gas station asked you about being a fighter or something. Is that right?'

'I was.'

'When?'

'Once upon a time.'

'Is this your house?'

'No. Not really. Who are you again?' he said and then he turned the key to the ignition. But the truck did not crank. He pulled back the key and then tried again. The engine strained and he pumped the gas but it did not catch and smoke began to seep through the front grille.

'You're gonna need a ride,' she said.

'Stupid ass motel mechanic,' he said and he slammed his fist against the top of the steering wheel and as his temper rose he felt a surge in his headache. He rubbed at the back of his neck. You got to be kidding me, he thought and he imagined the man in the bathrobe laid up on the bed in his motel room. Watching television. Laughing about Jack believing he was a capable mechanic. He looked across the driveway to her truck. 'Yeah. I guess I am.'

'Where to?'

'A nursing home on the other side of town.'

'I'll take you if you'll let me ask you some questions,' she said.

'I don't understand whatever it is you think you need to be asking me but if it'll get me where I'm going then fine.'

He pushed open the truck door and got out with the jewelry box and the lockbox and the notebook.

'You're forgetting something,' she said and she pointed at the Bible.

'Hold this,' he said and he handed her the boxes and notebook.

He opened the Bible and took out the notice of sale. He read it over again and then stuck it back inside the Bible and brought it along. They climbed in her pickup and she circled in the yard and when they came to the end of the driveway he told her to turn left.

He picked up the pack of cigarettes from on top of the dashboard and took one out and he found a lighter in the cupholder between the seats. He then pointed ahead and told her to take the right up there at that old café. He turned on the radio but she reached down and clicked it off.

'I'm serious,' she said. 'Can you listen now?'

They came to the small redbrick building with *MaMaw's Café* painted above the front door and Annette turned. Jack said you can ask me whatever but that doesn't mean I'll have an answer. He sucked on the cigarette and then he reached out and laid his hands on the dashboard and said stop.

'What is it?'

'Stop. Just pull over,' he said and he tossed the cigarette out the window. He had been eating Tylenol and trying to salvage that last of the pills for what his mind and body would suffer later in the night but the Tylenol was no match for what lived inside. The pain sharp between his shoulder blades and sharp in the back of his neck and he bent and pressed his forehead against the dash and said pull in over there and get me some water. Please right now. His back and legs clenching in small convulsions and she did not argue. She stopped in the parking lot of the café and hurried in and returned with a cup of water and he pulled two red pills from his pocket. Took the cup with a shaky hand and swallowed the pills. Drank the water and dropped the cup on the floorboard.

'Don't drive,' he said.

'Are you all right?'

'No. Just don't move.'

He wrapped his hands around his throat and pressed his fingers into the back of his neck as if trying to cut off the pain. He pressed against the top of his vertebra and something like a growl came from his throat. She wanted to do something but he had said don't move. So she watched him writhe and listened to his stunted breathing. Her hand on his shoulder. Wanting to ask what she could do but knowing he couldn't answer. He only rocked with his hands pressing against his head and she got out of the truck and went back inside. Got a plastic bag filled with ice and when she returned he had stopped rocking. She reached inside the open window and held the ice against the back of his neck as he whispered oh God.

He then moved his hands from his head and took the ice from her. Placed it on top of his head and leaned back in the seat. Annette lit a cigarette and began to pace across the parking lot, smoking and kicking at rocks and preaching to herself in rhythms of assurance and faith. One step has led you to the next and to the next and here you are and there is something here larger than anything you have seen or done before. Something. This is no strip club and this is no carnival. This is something beyond your own understanding. The jewelry box and the lockbox and the notebook and the truck and the old fighter in the Delta with a name that meant something. She looked at him through the window. You could be on the edge of some miracle. Or he could just be some junkie or worse and here you are the fool. Chasing when you should be running away. And then she cursed her own lack of conviction and she situated herself on her own front pew and waited for whatever was burning inside of him to subside long enough for her to ask her questions.

'My name is Annette,' she whispered. Practicing the way it sounded. Imagining her mother having sent a note or a photo of a baby with her name scribbled across the back to the man her mother only pretended not to remember. Imagining the magic of the four words once he heard them. The pain falling from his face when she said my name is Annette. She paced and whispered the words and watched him and waited and in the doctrine of her mind this would do it. He would recognize her name and realize who she was and a new day would begin.

He finally calmed. His arm resting in the open window and his head leaning on his arm. Eyes closed. The pain lessened to the point where he could be still.

She got in the truck and asked if he was okay. He lifted his head and nodded.

'Do you want to keep going?'

'Yeah.'

She drove slowly across the parking lot and out onto the road. Up ahead two tractors crept along and she passed them and asked if he could talk again.

'No,' he said. His heavy eyes. His bruised face from the wreck. The strained expression.

'Just let me help you then.'

'Help me do what?'

'Whatever you need. Are we almost there?'

'Yeah. Not far.'

Along the roadside teenagers held up signs that read FREE CARWASH and they waved cars toward the parking lot of a grocery store. At a rare red light a log truck had shorted a right turn and its back wheels had crushed a curb. The traffic waited while a city crew shoveled the broken concrete onto the back of a flatbed. Jack squinted but then moved his eyes over to Annette. Up and down her arms and up and down her legs. He saw there was addiction in her like there was in him. He wished his own could have at least been so artistic. The crew shoveled away the last of the concrete and the line of vehicles moved through the intersection.

'Swing in up there,' he said. 'The next driveway on the right.'

She turned in at the sign for Friendship Village Retirement Care. Followed the driveway to the front and looped through the parking lot. She parked in front of the row of hedges that lined the beige brick building and turned off the ignition. She then hurried around to Jack's door and put out her hand and he took it. He eased out and stood hunched, holding the boxes and the notebook and she kept fingers to his elbow and walked with him until they were inside.

'I got it from here,' he said. 'Unless you can wait a little while and give me another ride.'

You still haven't answered my questions, she wanted to say. But he had the roughworn look of a man who was either squeezed right in the middle of hard and unforgiving things or at the end of some hellish journey. His pain and the deliberate nature when he walked or talked. The things he carried. And the necessity of coming to this place where they could only be someone he loved who did not have much longer to remain in this world. So she didn't interrupt whatever he had to do with her own curiosity. He won't run away, she thought. I've waited this long. I can wait until he's done.

'That's fine,' she said. 'Whenever you're ready.'

'I can't believe somebody who looks like you has got nothing better to do,' he said and then he started toward the freshly mopped hallway. She shuffled along with him, glancing at the photographs and crayon drawings that decorated the doors of

the residents. He dropped the notebook and she picked it up.
Worn and tattered. Stained with coffee. He took it from her and
they passed two more rooms and then he stopped. The door
was open a few inches and Jack nudged it and they moved inside.
Only the light through the blinds and the steady beep from a
monitor next to the bed. He set the boxes and notebook on the
floor and then he slid a chair over close to her. Her eyes were
halfshut and she was mumbling in a dream. A stream of words
that did not connect and she rolled her head on the pillow. He
patted her hand and said it will be okay, Maryann. It's okay.

24

JACK STROKED THE TOP OF MARYANN'S hand and whispered to her and she quieted. Her head became still. Her eyes opened and she seemed to try and smile at him. Annette stood back from the bed in the corner of the room. Not expecting someone so frail and as he touched her wilted hand and whispered assurances, she realized she was an intruder.

She stepped back into the hallway. Walked and found the cafeteria and she poured coffee into a white foam cup. Residents had begun to come into the cafeteria for dinner, moving with canes and walkers. Some in wheelchairs. Women wearing light blue scrubs helped them to tables and into chairs. Brought trays with plates of food and cartons of milk to those who couldn't get it themselves. A wave of selfconsciousness came over her. She sipped the coffee and with her other hand rubbed at her bare arms and thighs. Wanted to be wearing long sleeves and jeans. Wanted the eyes, for once, to stay off her.

She left the cafeteria and returned to Maryann's door. Put her back against the hallway wall and slid down. Her knees up and her eyes on the photograph on the door across from her. A wrinkled little man sitting in a chair in the middle and his children and grandchildren and great grandchildren surrounding him.

So many of them that they leaned and crammed together to fit the entire family into the photo.

A cough from inside the room made her get to her feet. Jack let out big hacks and gasped for breath and she peeked through the door crack. Saw him stand from the bed and drink some water and get it together and then he wiped the side of his face. He then picked up the lockbox from the floor and he sat back down in the chair next to the bed. Opened the lockbox and lifted out a stack of letters.

He pushed her hair away from her eyes. The blond gone from it and the gray gone from it. But still so long and thick, laying across her neck and shoulders like winding white trails of the past. He straightened the gown around her neck. And then he took an envelope. Opened it and removed the letter inside. And he began to read to her. He read slowly and patiently as if to make certain that each word found its way inside. When he was done with the first letter he laid it aside and then he opened the next one and he would read them all to her as if each letter were some sort of handwritten currency that could buy back the memories of her life. The emotions. The victories and the defeats. He read as if he could use the sentiments of the voice from long ago to purchase the parts to make her whole again. If only for a moment. She sometimes watched him and he believed that deep beyond her gray eyes she knew who he was and what he had found and what he was trying to share with her. Subtle glints of recognition, eyes that shifted in the shaded sunlight and said I can feel it all again and I am not dead yet. I can feel it all right there where it hurt before. And then she would look away as if there were images painted across the cream-colored wall, colors and shapes and faces that only she could see. Some subconscious collage of a life that existed now only in the endless realm of the imagination. He read without hurry and lifted his eyes to watch her and he wanted to stop and ask her about it all. Tell me. Tell me about her. Tell me why you didn't go and were the hands that held you back visible or invisible or both. Or did they finally belong to me. But he didn't pause to ask and he stayed in her story and when she finally closed her eyes he kept on reading. And as he read he saw her life but in another part of his mind he saw himself digging two postholes out among the wild magnolias next to the abandoned chapel, the place where he had watched her walk and whisper to herself. He saw him himself sinking two posts in concrete and nailing a strip of lattice between the posts and planting wisteria vines that in the years to come would grow and weave through the lattice and deliver soft purple blossoms that would sway in the Delta wind and he saw himself digging her grave and burying her there beneath the blossoms, in the rich soil that in life had held her so tightly.

She sat back down on the floor and didn't know what she was listening to. Only that it was important. Only that it was full of guts and heart and she was hypnotized by the tenderness and defeat and hope all wound together and the more he read the more heartache she felt. Heartache for the person who had written the words and heartache for who they were written to and heartache for the man who sat reading them. Something fallen in his voice.

And then there was a pause. Several minutes of silence. She rose to her feet and leaned her head closer to the opening in the doorway. No more words and no more movement. She pushed open the door and his head was lying on the bed next to her and his eyes closed. The letters and envelopes scattered across the bed and the lockbox open and empty. She moved quietly into the room. The jewelry box and the notebook were on the floor at the foot of the bed and she knelt and picked up the notebook and then crept back into the hallway.

She began to turn the pages and it was as if she were trying to make sense of a foreign language. Smatterings of directions. Fragments of sentences. Rudimentary addition and subtraction. Names of people and places scattered across the pages in a reckless handwriting. The corners of some of the pages singed from cigarette burns. What she could only believe to be dried blood smeared across the inside flap. She turned through the pages and imagined his chaos and wondered if her own life of flight may someday come to this.

There was movement inside the room and she closed the notebook. Peeked around the door and Jack had raised his head. He gathered the letters and envelopes and set them inside the lockbox. He closed the lid and set it next to the woman in the bed. Lifted her hand and laid it on top of the box. And then Annette listened as he began his confession.

Your family's land is gone. All of it. To where I don't fucking know, Maryann. I wish I did. But it's gone and the house is next in only a few more days. All I can do is tell you I'm sorry but even saying it sounds like bullshit. The messed up part of me swore I'd get it all back but the story never ends that way. I'm a junkie and a drunk and there's no other way around it. I'm never going to be off the pills because it's just not possible. That's not who you raised me to be but that's who I am. Worse than all that I haven't been here to see you as much as I should have. You treated me like your son. But I'm not a good one and I hope like hell you didn't stay here because of me. I want to tell you I'm going to be back here. I want to come back and sit with you and read the letters but I can't say for sure that will happen either. I gotta go fight, Maryann. I'm gonna take your jewelry and beg like a dog but I don't think it'll matter. And it's gonna be a goddamn bad one. They're all goddamn bad but nothing like this is gonna be. I wish I had something better to tell you about but I don't.

Outside the door Annette held the notebook next to her chest. When this day began she was sitting at a café, deciding to drive away. Deciding to be alone again. Trusting her church to lead her in the right direction. And now this. She could not decide if she was putting together pieces to some fateful puzzle or if she had simply fallen into this man's mess because of her own need.

She pushed open the door and stepped inside. She set the notebook on top of the dresser and then she knelt at the foot of the bed. Folded her arms on top of the rail.

'Who is she?' she said.

'Maryann,' he answered. 'My mother.'

'How much longer do you think she has?'

Jack shrugged. 'A minute. A week. I don't know,' he said.

They spoke in low, almost reverent voices. Maryann shifted and a quick and highpitched sound came from her parted lips. She lifted her hand and pointed at the plastic pitcher of water on the tray table. Jack filled the cup and stuck a straw in it and held it to her lips. She sipped and then laid her head back.

'She looks like she was a good woman.'

'She was. She didn't have to do nothing for me.'

'What do you mean?'

'She's my foster mother. Took me in when I was hard to handle and never looked back,' he said.

Annette raised her folded arms from the bedrail. She stared at him as he stared at Maryann. The robotic rhythm of the beeps from the machines. The falling light of a late afternoon through the blinds. He looks like a wounded animal, she thought. A wounded animal ready to wander off into the woods and find a comfortable place to die. And then she turned her eyes again to Maryann. The small lumps of her knees and feet underneath the blanket. The pronounced cheekbones from her fading expression, an expression that seemed to be drifting between worlds. She admired her long white hair and her hands that rested still and peaceful and then Annette saw herself lying there. Time having robbed her of the natural gifts she now possessed and her own wandering having led her to a similar room in a similar place except that there would be no one there to sit with her. No one to say goodbye to. And she thought of Baron walking alone down that country road in Arkansas in the midst of a starstruck night and she thought of her own mother wherever she was and she imagined the highways before her that she would drive as she kept running away from one thing and to another and something moved inside her that was strange and strong as she wanted this moment to be the beginning of something that would not end.

'Did you ever know a woman named Sally Magee?' she asked.

Jack touched the straw to Maryann's lips once more and then said 'What am I supposed to know her from?'

'From twenty-five years ago,' she said.

'Is this what you've been waiting around to ask me?'

'Yeah. I hate to do it sitting here but I need to know.'

Jack set the straw on the tray table. Stood from the chair and grabbed the notebook from the top of the dresser. 'Come on,' he said and he waved her toward the door.

In the hallway he opened the notebook.

'What is that?' she asked.

'Just something I carry with me. Nobody is in here from that long ago but I'll look. Why should I know her?'

'My name is Annette. And she's my mother,' she said and she folded her arms. Looked down at her feet and then up again.

He then closed the notebook and held it up. 'What were you doing with it?' he asked.

'Just looking. There's nothing in there to understand.'

'Did you see her name?'

'I told you. I can't understand any of it.'

'I can't do this right now.'

'This is a shitty time to be asking you this but I can't help it. You showed up at the gas station. That woman said you were a fighter and that your name meant butcher. Those are the only two things Sally ever told me about my father. He's a fighter and his name means something. And she said you were from the Delta and we're in the Delta. I don't have a choice but to ask.'

A nurse came out of a room at the end of the hallway and walked toward them. They hushed and waited for her to pass.

'Is all that you said to her true?' she asked.

He nodded.

'Why do you have to fight tonight?'

He lowered his head for an instant and raised it again. 'Come with me,' he said.

They passed along the hallway and through the great room and exited the front door. In the parking lot he turned to her and handed her the notebook and said I know what you're looking for and I even can understand why you're looking and if there is an answer it's in here. Search it again. It's chicken scratch but if you really want to know you'll go through it again. She took it from him and sat down on the curb next to a large terracotta pot overflowing with a healthy fern. Jack lit a cigarette and paced around the lot while she turned the pages. She was more careful this time, with careful and studying eyes.

He walked back over to her and flicked away the cigarette.

'You really want to know why I have to fight tonight?' he asked.

She looked up from the notebook and said yes. He reached into his pocket and pulled out the last pill. Stuck it in his mouth and swallowed. And then he told her about the headaches and about his bad habit of creating more bad habits and he explained that this was why he carried around the notebook. Because it's getting worse and there's no turning back. He had not talked to anyone in a long time and he began to empty himself and he told her about Big Momma Sweet and who she was and what he owed her and because he didn't have the money his only choice was to fight. Fight or have a blade pulled across his throat. Right after they branded him with a dollar sign. I had it, he said. I was on my way. And then I was gonna try to figure out about the house and then he trailed off after mentioning the house. He held his hands up and turned them around as if seeing them for the first time and then he closed his fingers and made fists. Moved them slowly to his face and pressed the knuckles against his cheeks. When he moved his fists away there were red imprints on his skin and then he let go of the fists and held his hands open. Looked into his own palms as the twilight settled around them and the anxiety relented on his scarred face. His eyes softening as if he had come to some resolution. An acceptance of fate.

'You should probably go,' he said. 'Even if you only believe half of what you've seen here, you can figure out it's best to get far away from me.'

She closed the notebook and stood.

'What house are you talking about? The one where I found you? That big white one?'

'It doesn't matter.'

'And what happened to the money?' she said.

'That doesn't matter either.'

She handed him back the notebook and said I know about the wreck. I don't know where you were when we came up on it and the further me and you go along I don't really care. But there is a great big world spinning around and sometimes it spins against you. Sometimes it spins with you. And sometimes it spins us right into what we need. That jackass who stuck his knife in my tire today slammed us right into each other, Jack. Without him I would have been gone a long way from here by now. But he did stick the knife in my tire. And then I heard what the woman said about you and I followed you to your house because you are the only man I've ever come across who I thought had a prayer of being my father. It's a longshot. I know. Most things are. God knows I've imagined what you might look like or be like and God knows you're way beyond any of that.

'You haven't imagined me because you don't know who I am. And neither do I,' he said. 'I was a fighter but I'm not anymore. You've heard what all I said to Maryann. You see me. I've dug a grave for myself and I've been trying to figure a way out but it ain't gonna happen and before this night is over there's a fair chance I'll be laying in it. Your story about the world spinning around can't change any of that.'

She turned and walked across the parking lot and to the truck. She opened the door and reached underneath the seat and pulled out the casino envelope that held his money. Her tattooed body marching to the rhythm of her own gospel hymn as she strode over to him and held it out and said whether you understand it or not I was sent here to help you. I've been led right down into the grave with you by some force stronger than all of us. But what I'm doing now is standing below you in the bottom so I can shove you out. I don't know if I'm your daughter but I am your angel and I bet you never thought of an angel doing such dirty work. But I'm no angel from heaven. It doesn't matter where I came from, only that I'm here.

25

THE LAND OF BIG MOMMA SWEET was a place of mythical violence. Since late Wednesday night when Jack had taken Skelly's body out into the rain to bury, Big Momma Sweet had spread her word through the jukejoints and barrooms and gambling houses of the Mississippi Delta like a fatal disease. Big Momma Sweet is having a fight. A big fight with no betting limit. And it's Jack Boucher, the most unpredictable son of a bitch you ever saw put his fists up. Two days from now on Friday night. Cash your damn paychecks and come on.

He's too old, some of them said.

I thought he was dead, some of them said.

He looks like he crawled out of a landfill, some of them said.

I wouldn't bet on his ass, some of them said.

I wouldn't bet against him, some of them said.

The crowd came early. Arriving at noon and sitting on tailgates and drinking beer from their coolers. Comparing rifles and pistols. The card games and the prostitutes started up in the middle of the afternoon and the music bumped and echoed out through the trees. They knelt around card tables because all the seats were full and when Big Momma Sweet told her men to cut them off at the door the gambling spilled out into the sunlight.

Cards dealt across hoods and dice skipping across the dirt. Big Momma Sweet made sure she had plenty of women and they all danced and howled and satisfied every lust that money could buy in prelude to the vicious night. Some brought grills in their truck beds and coolers packed with venison and pork and the smell of charcoal and meat wafted in the humid air in breaking gray clouds. Some wandered over to the open-air barn and admired vehicles they had once owned but had been forced to turn the titles over to Big Momma Sweet to settle their debts.

A moonshiner sold glass jars from wooden crates packed with hay and he passed over half of every dollar that touched his hand to Ern, who sat next to him in a lawn chair much too small for his bulky frame. The day wore on and more trucks and cars and motorcycles and fourwheelers followed the dirt road out to this place by the river where there was no law but what Big Momma Sweet decreed. And the crowd grew larger and drunker as the sun fell from the sky. The women danced on the porch and they danced outside and the amps were turned higher and the drums beat faster. Shoving and shouting matches broke out over which side of the dice was up or when tough guys recognized one another from not yet forgotten barroom brawls. The moon showed itself before the sun disappeared as if the earth could not decide which direction to spin. And then Big Momma Sweet sent her boys out with torches that were driven into the ground and the crowd howled and barked when the torches were lit because night would be there soon.

Big Momma Sweet stood in the window of her raised cabin. Her wild hair pushed straight up as if trying to escape from her head. The pipe in her hand and her meaty arms folded as she surveyed the scene like a goddess of vice and she wondered if Jack would show up.

She had set the odds of the fight at 7-to-1. Jack the heavy underdog. She set it at 7-to-1 because she liked the number seven and if the odds were greater against Jack they would have been certain she had arranged for him to win. Any lower and the only question would be what round Jack would go down. With the odds at 7-to-1 there was uncertainty and debate and she had long known this was how you made your money on the fights.

Jack's opponent paced across the other side of the cabin. Shirtless and his hard shoulders and chest damp with a nervous sweat. She drew on the pipe and told him to sit down. You're going to walk a hole in my floor. Save whatever you got for tonight. It'll get here like it always does.

He called himself Ax. His hair cut in a mohawk and veins bulging from his biceps. His two front teeth missing and HELL tattooed across the four fingers of his right hand and FIRE tattooed across the four fingers of his left. He paced and bounced on his tiptoes because his time had come. He had been the one called to fight Jack Boucher and he was going to be the one to finish him. In a place where they screamed and cussed and spit and cried out with savage shrieks for the bleeding and the breaking. He could think of nothing other than the night to come and what he was going to do to make them talk about him forever. The night he destroyed a legend.

Big feet sounded on the stairs and the door opened. Ern came in with a wad of cash. He plopped down on the sofa. Lit a clove cigarette and began to straighten the bills.

'I ain't never seen this many fools out here,' he said.

'Nope,' Big Momma answered and she sat down with him. 'Only issue being we're still missing the biggest fool of all.'

'You think he's run off?'

'If he knows what's good for him,' Ax said.

'Ain't nobody talking to you,' Big Momma said. 'You better

hope he shows or I might toss you out there in the dog pit just for fun.'

The ice shifted in the silver bin in the corner and Big Momma pointed to it. Told Ax to do something worth a damn and grab me one of them beers. He crossed the room and pulled a can from the ice.

'Get one for yourself,' she said. 'It'll help you ease up.'

'I didn't come here to ease up.'

'Except that I just told you to. You're driving me crazy. Go on in the other room. I can't stand the sight of you right now.'

He popped the top on the beer and followed her finger out of the room.

'Where'd you find him?' Ern ask. 'Motherfucker looks nasty.'

'He is nasty. Just what we need for a night like this.'

Big Ern grinned and counted the moonshine money. Fives and tens in one stack and singles in another. 'You showed that big boy to anybody yet?' he asked.

'I was thinking of walking him out on deck. Soon as they get a glimpse every eye in this place will decide it has seen the victor.'

'Yep,' Ern said and he leaned back. 'Except won't nobody trust their eyes.'

'That's right.'

'And they're gonna think about it too hard. Think you're up to something.'

'That's right, too.'

'And that's when the money will roll in on Jack and that's when Big Momma makes the big pile.'

'You just about got it figured out.'

'But they ain't seen Jack. And if they do before the fight I'm guessing he will not impress too many dollar bills.'

'No. And that's why I been making a consideration,' she said and took a long drink from the beer. Wrapped her hand around the cold can and then held it to her forehead.

'A consideration of what?'

'You laid your eyes on Jack the other night. He looks like he might fall over if the wind hit him right. And I heard he didn't do much of nothing down in Vidalia except throw a few punches and cover up and wait to drop and get paid.'

'Yeah. So?'

'So. We got a damn animal to fight him. My opinion is if Jack shows, there's a decent chance he won't make it through the night. Truth is, I used to like Jack but he has come to the end of his road. He's as likely to get killed from this fight as he is to survive. And I can't see no reason not to prosper. I'm guessing the crowd outside might be interested in a side bet. We'll call it live or die.'

'Damn, Big Momma,' Ern said.

She sipped on the beer. Strolled around the sofa.

'We'll take two bets,' she said. 'One on the odds of the fight. And then another on whether or not Jack lives through it.'

'Holy shit. We ain't never done nothing like that.'

'We never had the opportunity. Don't say nothing to that lug in there or Jack. If and when he gets here we'll let it be known. The crowd will be in a damn frenzy and I'm guessing we'll need a wheelbarrow to haul bets on Jack surviving.'

'Even money?'

'Even money. Win or lose. We might even be doing Jack a favor. He's got the look of dying in an alley somewhere. At least this way we'll give him a decent burial right here at home.'

'So this is anything goes?'

'Anything,' she said and took the clove cigarette from between his fingers. Puckered her lips and smoked. 'Give them what they want.'

26

HIS EYES HAD OPENED WIDE WHEN he recognized the envelope and all her talk of angels and destiny solidified right before him as they stood together in the parking lot of the nursing home. He stood dumbfounded by the deliverance until he finally took it from her and asked how in the hell did you get this?

She told him about the carnival driving through the night and coming upon the scene of the wreck. About finding the money and leaving the body. She then explained Ricky Joe at the gas station and how he had seen them find the envelope at the wreck though he didn't know exactly what it was and he had seen the body. Baron had given the money to her for safekeeping and she had decided to take it and go wherever her church was leading her right about the time the woman came out of the gas station and recognized him. And then he drove past in the truck from the wreck. Baron headed to get the carnival broken down and get the hell out of town but she followed Jack.

He listened and as she talked her eyes shined in the last light of day. Two suns holding on to the horizon. She was a believer. In what, he didn't exactly know. But with the money in his hands he could not think of a reason not to trust in what she had to say.

'Wait right here,' he said. He returned inside the nursing home and to Maryann's room. He took the notebook and jewelry box and lockbox of letters and stuck them in the bottom drawer of the dresser. Then he kissed Maryann's forehead and said I'll be right back. He then hurried out and back to Annette and said let's go.

'Where?'

'I'll explain on the way.'

They left the nursing home and stopped for more cigarettes and then they drove away from town, out onto the straight and empty highway and he began to tell the story. His dilemma with Big Momma Sweet and how they had helped each other make a few dollars but she wasn't on his side anymore. That he needed twelve thousand to get Big Momma off his ass but the wreck ruined that plan. Now he'd have to fight even though he told her he didn't have that kind of fight left in him and he was going to offer what was in the jewelry box.

'But now, you changed all that,' he said.

They smoked and drove on. The road rough and patched. A steady weakening of day into night and something soft and violet caressed the land. He laid his head on the headrest, stared at himself in the sideview mirror. Stared at the wrinkles and scars. His eyes heavy with the lack of sleep and the pills and for the moment his body had found a painless position and he imagined he was being driven toward some protective realm by an angelic chauffeur. A falling of light. A falling of pain. A dark horizon waiting at the end of the highway to accept his spirit into a timeless space and judge it for no more than what it was. He rolled his head to the side and studied Annette. Her hair in the wind and her deadset eyes and her unwavering belief that today she had stumbled upon something beautiful. That she was part of some miracle and he couldn't think of any other way to describe it himself and when this miracle was over and tomorrow arrived he didn't want to be there when she realized he was only a walking shell of a man. A man unable. And that her God had lied to her. Or maybe she is an angel, he thought. Or magic. Or is she even real and is this a dream and maybe I've already been to see Big Momma and I've already had the fight and I've been knocked so far out of my own mind that I'm stuck in some unconscious creation of a happy ending. Like I hope Maryann's mind is doing for her right now.

He touched the fresh burn on his neck from the branding iron. Raised and tender. Touched the scars of his face and his crooked nose and then he searched for himself in her profile. In the slant of the nose or in the bend of the mouth. She sucked on a cigarette and he watched her cheeks and chin and the way she squinted when the smoke curled past her eyes and he tried to find a resemblance to a younger, smoothskinned Jack Boucher. Figured her mother was a looker with the way Annette turned out. The tattoos wrapping her arms and legs and chest and she wore her story all over her body. Just like me, he thought.

And what if she is right? What if twenty-something years ago in one of those towns after one of those fights you walked out the door of one of those bars with one of those women who believed you were the hotshot you claimed to be? What if you and that woman climbed all over each other with the sheets ripped from the bed and then what if nine months later a baby was born? A girl. And what if she grew up and never laid eyes on her father but never let go of what she knew about him? He was a fighter. And what if she ended up with a truckload of tattoos and then what if one day she crossed the Delta as the sultry sideshow for some vagabond carnival and what if every damn thing happened just like she believes it happened and here she is? And here you are. Somehow still alive long enough for her to find you. What if she is the savior she claims to be?

He picked up the motel Bible. Opened it and took out the notice of sale. He believed the Bible to be full of promises though he had never bothered to find out where to look for them and as he unfolded the notice he wondered if there may be one last thing to ask for. There wasn't enough light to read but he ran his fingertips across the page and felt the certainty of the words and he folded the notice and tucked it back into the Bible.

And then it was night. The miles thumping and the final light disappearing and his mind turned toward the possibility of the impossible. His own blood did remain in the world but it did not run through the veins of those who put his small feet into the dirt and drove away from the Salvation Army store so many years ago but it flowed through the veins of a young woman. A young woman led by her own conviction. A young woman who had followed him unconcerned about the risk because she believed him to be something to her and now she was going to save him. He looked across the flatlands and in the distance he felt as if he could see the ends of the earth. And it was always in the veil of night when he felt like anything was possible.

27

THE NARROW ROAD MADE A LONG bend to the left and then another long bend to the right. Small breaks of river flowed into clumps of hardwoods and gathered in shaded, murky pools of muddy water. They crossed over a levee and then passed cut piles of forgotten and decaying timber and then the road trailed in one last long curve. And they saw it.

The vehicles spread across the field and the lights of the shacks.

'Holy shit,' Annette said. 'All of these people are here for you?'

Jack raised from the seat. Pressed his hands together. He had what he owed but he looked at the crowd and wondered if she would even let him buy his way out there was so much to be made on a night like this. They rolled up the truck windows and drove slowly through the scene. Men sitting on open tailgates and leaning against trucks stared and Jack held his hand up to cover the side of his face not wanting to be recognized. The laughter of women and the big voices of men and a kickdrum beat like the racing pulse of anticipation. The orange flames of the torches waved against the fallen night and on the other side of the shacks the lights that hung from the steel rafters of the metal barn shined down on the cage at odd angles, the tall corner poles falling into shadows of crosses on the smooth dirt of the fighting pit. A fire burned in a circle of stones next to the cage where the brand would heat and glow like the sun, preparing for him to lose.

'Get as close as you can get to the cabin on stilts,' he said.

Men stood in the road smoking and drinking moonshine and were slow to move to the side. They whistled when they caught sight of Annette and Jack kept his hand across his face, watching between his fingers. She drove carefully and nudged between a cluster of motorcycles only a few steps away from the bottom of the cabin stairs. On each side of the stairs stood hefty, watchful men. One held an aluminum baseball bat. The other stood with folded arms and the handle of a pistol stuck out of the front of his pants.

Jack took the envelope from between his legs and held it with both hands.

'I'll be right back.'

'I'll go with you,' she said.

'You don't want to go in there.'

'I don't really want to stay out here either.'

'Just lock the doors. And keep it running.'

He opened the door of the cabin and stepped inside. Big Momma Sweet sat on the couch and she rolled her eyes over to him.

'Right on time,' she said.

Ern was on a stool next to the table of knives. A door opened from the hallway and Ax came into the room. His skin glistened with sweat and he seemed to be chewing at the inside of his mouth.

'Who's the pretty boy?' Jack said. He then moved over toward the couch and he dropped the envelope onto the coffee table next to her propped feet.

'What's that supposed to be?' she said and she sat up.

'It's what I owe you. Every nickel. Twelve large. Ern can count it if you think he can go that high.'

'You yellow dog,' the young opponent said.

'Fuck you.'

'Hey,' Big Momma Sweet yelled at Ax. 'How many times I got to tell you to stop talking? This don't concern you none.'

'I came out here for a fight.'

'Get out that door,' she said.

'That was my deal.'

'You'll get to fight something.'

Ern moved to the sofa and pulled a billy club from beneath a cushion and he raised it toward Ax. Said I know you ain't talking back to Big Momma. I know it. And all I got to do is whistle and I'll have a gang of boys in here to drag you out to the river. You hearing this?

The young man turned red and his broad shoulders moved nervously up and down. He nodded and he walked across the cabin, eyes on Jack. And then he went out and waited on the deck. Ern closed the door behind him.

'You couldn't find nobody bigger than him?' Jack asked.

'The bigger they are, Jack. Ain't that how it goes?'

'That's how it goes but it makes no difference. There's the money. I told you I had it.'

'And it just came back from the dead?'

'Something like that. Go ahead. Count it.'

'I don't need to.'

'Good. Then I'm gone.'

'Gone where?'

'Away from here,' he said and moved toward the door. Ern stood in front and didn't move.

'This ain't how it works, Big Momma,' Jack said. 'Even is even.'

She tapped her finger on top of the envelope. Lifted her pipe and a box of matches from the table. Then she stood and strode around the room in thoughtful steps with the unlit pipe dangling between her fingers.

'We ain't gonna mess with you,' she said and she waved Ern to the side. 'You paid. You're free. But look out the window before you head for the door. Come on and look.'

Jack stepped over to the window. Pulled a beer from the silver bin. Opened it and drank and looked out across the spectacle. He then turned from the window and drank again and said there you go. I did it.

'Must be five hundred strong,' she said.

'I don't care.'

'You might could make some money.'

'I know and I still don't care.'

'That ain't the Jack I know.'

'Well,' he said. 'I've been rehabilitated.'

'There ain't no such thing. Or else I'd be out of business,' she said.

Jack drank from the beer again. Licked his lips and looked at Ern and then back to her. 'I'm going now,' he said.

'You're out of one hole,' she said. 'But not the other. I know what you still need. So do you. I hear the big house goes up for auction first of the week and that woman's still laying in the old folks home.'

'Yeah. I know. I also know you won't pay me thirty grand to fight that big son of a bitch.'

'You're right. I won't.'

Ern waited. Jack waited. Then Big Momma Sweet told Ern to get out of the way and he stepped to the side. Jack finished off the beer.

'But the odds are seven to one,' she said.

'I already told you. I don't care,' he answered and he tossed the empty can into the bin. Then he walked past Ern and out the door and Ern closed it behind him.

The floodlights shined from the corners of the cabin and when Ax came onto the deck some in the crowd below had noticed him and they gawked at his wide shoulders and arms like tree limbs. He stalked along the cabin deck, slapping at his own face and running his hand across the mohawk and flexing his shoulders and chest as more gathered below. But then he had seen Jack move over to the window and look out and he stopped. Stood next to the window and listened to what he and Big Momma Sweet were saying. And he heard her tell him the odds of the fight and he heard Jack say no thanks.

He now leaned against the deck railing, the intensity draining from him. The crowd calling to him but he ignored the noise. Then the door opened and Jack came out. When the crowd saw Jack standing next to Ax they pointed and laughed and some grimaced. Ax a head taller than Jack. Muscled and glistening in the floodlights. Jack ignored Ax as some of the voices from the crowd began to call out to Jack and some cried insults and some made jokes but it was only the sounds of the night to him. Nothing he hadn't heard before. He had started down the cabin stairs when Ax moved across the deck and in a low and threatening voice he said you're lucky, old man.

Jack stopped midway on the staircase and looked over his

shoulder. The two words like two bullets fired at him from the blurry years gone by.

'What?'

'You heard me.'

From below Annette rolled down the window and called for him to come on.

'I don't think I did,' Jack said.

'I said you're lucky, old man. And you better get your old ass out of here while you can still walk and talk.'

Jack paused. The crowd began to rumble as it watched the two men. And then their voices charged the night, a twisted fury of shouts and bellows and they all wanted the same thing. They all wanted the line to be crossed where there was no return.

He listened to them. Moved his eyes from the young man and looked out into the valley of night. A single bright star shined in the low sky and in this star he seemed to see everything. This brilliant rebel diamond against the backdrop of infinity.

He then descended the stairs. Moved between the men on guard. Moved between the motorcycles and to the truck. Annette leaned over and pulled the lock. He opened the door but did not climb in. He leaned across and asked if she had something to write with. She stuck her fingers into a small shelf beneath the radio and handed him a pen.

'What is it?' she said.

On the back of his hand he multiplied twelve and seven and it came out to eighty-four. Plenty, he whispered.

'Would you tell me what you're doing?'

'Figuring the odds.'

'Of what?'

'Of the fight. It's seven-to-one against me.'

'Is that who you're supposed to be fighting right up there?' she asked and she pointed up the stairs.

'Yeah.'

'Then it should damn sure be way more than seven-to-one. Do you see the size of that son of a bitch?'

'I can get the house.'

'You can get a lot worse. Did you even give her the money?'

'She's got it.'

'Then let's go.'

'I know what you're thinking,' he said. 'But you have to know what I'm thinking too and you'd be better off if you didn't try to figure it out.'

'Jack. Get in. I'll take you back to Maryann.'

With the mention of Maryann's name he paused. Sat down inside the truck and closed the door. The crowd had moved around them now. Hands propped on the tailgate and hips leaning against the hood and the voices goading Jack, believing he was running away. Shouts of chicken shit and coward and he began to feel the rush. The spike of adrenaline that came from the energy of their cries and their money on the line and the chance of proving them all wrong. Annette tapped her hands on the steering wheel and said let's go. Please. Let's go. But he lowered his eyes. Held his hands between his knees and flexed his fingers. Listened to the shouts from the crowd and his blood surged and he felt the presence of this angel beside him and all that she had delivered and he believed in her because he needed something to believe in. There was only one voice now and it was the voice telling him you will never be here again. You will never be as close as this.

Annette reached over and put her hand on his shoulder and told him to say something. Tell me to crank the truck and go. Are you all right? He raised his eyes from his hands and they fell on the hawk on her thigh. Its sharp head and wings spread in a pose of predatory ascension. The memory of his first moments in the field and the hawk guiding him toward Maryann long gone but his eyes fell on the hawk and his mind searched it for familiarity, as if it was a word of a secret language he could almost understand.

There is only all or nothing, he thought. There is no in between.

'Just wait here,' he said. He closed the truck door and wrangled through the crowd and climbed back up the stairs. He then went inside the cabin and he walked over to the coffee table. The envelope had not moved and he picked it up and Big Momma and Ern stared at him.

'Seven to one.' he said. 'Right?'

Big Momma Sweet sucked on the pipe. 'Seven to one,' she said.

'I want to make a bet.'

'I don't know. You already paid up. I wonder if I can let you take it back. What you think, Ern?'

'I think that's the craziest fucking white boy I ever seen.'

'I reckon that means you can take it back then,' she said.

'Before I do, let's make sure we understand what twelve thousand multiplied by seven comes out to.'

'I'm aware,' she said.

'Can you cover it?'

'Don't be ridiculous.'

'Then I'm putting twelve thousand on myself. Pays eighty-four grand at the end.'

'That's good math, Jack. But while we're multiplying, we better try some subtraction too and make damn sure we understand what twelve thousand minus twelve thousand comes out to. Because when the clock strikes midnight, Cinderella, there won't be no more magic. If you lose you still owe me and if I don't get my money, you'll be laying by Skelly. And you'll be wearing my dollar sign when you get to where you're going so the devil will know you came from me.'

Jack nodded but something shifted in his eyes. There was no more weariness. No more caution. He dropped the envelope on the table and said we go to the cage right now.

Ax had moved into the doorway and he stood there wrenching his hands together and huffing and puffing like some deranged vessel of destruction.

'How about you, big boy? You ready now?' Big Momma asked him and she shook her head and cackled. Then Ern walked out and down the steps. Whispered to the two guards about the live or die side bet they were setting for Jack and he sent them out to spread it through the crowd. They're gonna ask you if it's a joke but it ain't no joke. And as the men moved out into the fueled crowd they discovered Ern was right. They didn't believe it. Live or die? But Big Momma's men confirmed and said if you don't believe us go ask Ern but in the end nobody needed to ask Ern. Some shook their heads and said I can't be part of this and they took their beers and headed for their vehicles. Others shook their heads and didn't want to be part of it but they headed for the cage anyway. And still others began only to try and figure out which side of the bet was the right one, hurrying to lay down their money on whether or not they believed Jack would rise from the cruel cage.

28

Annette watched Big Momma's men come down the stairs and move through the crowd. Saw the surprised expressions on the faces as some kind of news seemed to pass among them and there was more yelling and shouting. Hands slapped the roof of the truck and drunken eyes gave her final looks before the crowd began to migrate away from the cabin and out toward the shacks and the fighting pit. She waited with her hand on the door handle until the crowd drifted away and then she unlocked the door and got out. When Jack came down the stairs she met him at the bottom.

'You told me twenty times you can't fight and now you're fighting,' she said. 'Why couldn't you just pay the money you owed and get the hell out of here like you said you were going to do?'

'Because I can't leave her there. I can't die with that house on my conscience.'

'But you can't fight either. Jesus Christ, you were doubled over with a headache on the way to the nursing home.'

'I know all that so you might as well quit reminding me.'

'I swear to God,' she said and she shook her head nervously as she looked across this place. Two drunks stumbled into each other and fell to the ground. A woman stood in the open door of one of the shacks, smoking a cigar and wearing only boxer shorts and a cowboy hat. The bloodthirsty crowd moving toward the lights of the fighting pit, as if slogging to the end of some carnal pilgrimage. She shifted her feet and folded her arms and said I've been in some shitty places but this is the shittiest.

The door opened to the cabin and Big Momma Sweet came down the stairs with a shotgun resting on her shoulder and Ern followed behind holding the branding iron. The crowd noise was gaining strength as the night grew darker and Jack took off his shirt and tossed it onto the ground.

'I'm supposed to be dragging you out of your grave,' Annette said. 'Not helping to shove you in it.'

'You can't talk like that. Not now. This is done and there's only one way out and it leads right through that cage over there.'

He rolled his head and cracked his neck. Dropped and did a dozen push-ups and then rose to his feet and he stretched his arms over his head. Then he said just promise me that if I'm on the wrong end of this when it's over you'll hurry out of here. Don't wait around. Get to your truck and go but you have to swear you'll go to Maryann and promise me you'll sit with her. For a day or a few days or however long you can. Sit with her and read the letters to her. If you believe anything you've told me then swear to God you'll do this for me. Do you believe any of it? Because I need you to. I need you to believe it more than anything in this whole world.

'Yes,' she said. 'Yes. Yes dear God yes. I believe it. But that doesn't keep me from worrying you and me won't ever have another conversation. From worrying this crowd might eat itself and us with it. I want you to know who I am when this is over.'

He cracked his knuckles. Pulled back his arms and bent at the waist and stretched his back. He looked over her body and said if you have a deity on there somewhere we can pray to now would be a good time to point it out.

'I'm serious,' she said. 'I want you to know me. To know Maryann. I want you to be here.'

'I'm serious, too. Pray. Find something to pray to and pray like a lunatic. And you haven't promised me yet that you'll go back to Maryann and you have to do that before we say anything else. Before I get in that cage. I have to hear it.'

She stared at him for a moment. Wanting to make sure she would remember what he looked like before the fight began. And then she said I will go back and be with her. I promise.

He nodded. Felt the final release. And then he slapped his hands against his cheeks and against the sides of his head. Come on, he said. There is no more time to waste.

29

THE CROWD WAS FUNNELED INTO THE barn through a cattle gate. Big Momma's brutes stood at the gate and one of them waved a metal detector over each man passing into the fighting arena. No guns and no knives allowed. A wooden barrel sat next to the gate and if a weapon was lifted it was dropped into the barrel and became property of Big Momma Sweet.

But the crowd was familiar with the rule and the barrel stayed empty. They filed in and the two sets of bleachers filled up quickly and then the remaining crowd pushed close to the cage. A suffocating mass of the drunk and disturbed surrounding the cage on all four sides, the smell of whiskey and weed and cigarettes and the men pushing at one another, everyone wanting a better view.

Jack stood in one corner of the cage and Ax paced on the opposite side. Jack had picked up a folding chair along the way and he set it outside the fence in his corner. Annette sat in the chair with her arms crossed and her leg shaking nervously. A hand ran across her shoulder and she slapped it away and Jack stuck his finger through the cage and said to the scraggly man you better not touch her again.

'Shit,' the man said. 'I ain't worried about you. You ain't never coming out of there.'

The man's certainty jolted through Annette and she looked at Jack. He spit and then he walked to the side of the cage where Big Momma Sweet sat high in an umpire's chair she had Ern swipe from a tennis court. The single-barrel shotgun lay across her lap.

On the ground next to the tall legs of the chair a low fire burned and the brand of the dollar sign sat atop the red embers. Ern stood next to the pit with the billy club tucked under his arm and gave a salivating stare toward Jack.

'How are you gonna play this?' Jack asked.

'Same as always,' she said. 'I'm the bell ringer. When I ring it the fight starts. When I ring it again it's over. Ain't no rounds out here.'

The crowd surrounding them heard their exchange and shouts came straight and strong, heaping down on Jack. Get in there and fight. Live or die. Live or die. Random cries that slowly banded together and turned into a chant. Live or die.

Jack slapped his hands against the cage and moved back to his corner. Annette had her fingers wrapped through the chainlinks and he moved his face close to hers.

'You hear that?' she yelled.

'Don't listen.'

'They're yelling live or die, Jack,' she said and she began to look around as they chanted and raised their fists, a wildfire of energy.

'Look here,' he yelled.

She turned back to him with panicked eyes and said what the hell is going on? But he didn't answer and said look at me. Just look at me and let me look at you and focus. He wrapped his fingers around hers and wanted her to belong to him in this extraordinary moment and every moment after. Whether anything she had said or believed was true he wanted it all to be as he touched his fingers to hers and they held together between the chainlinks and he said my eyes in yours and tried to shut it all out. The cries of live or die and the smoke from the pit and the rabid faces surrounding the cage and the might and strength of the man in the other corner. He did not want to see it and hear it and he thought that if he stared at her then he could be somewhere else in these final moments. Keep your eyes in mine he said again and the world shrank into silence. He looked into the black circles of her eyes and deep inside he saw himself leaving this dark land and walking into the bank on a sunny day and paying the house out of foreclosure. He saw Maryann lying in a bed in her own bedroom. Next to the window. Her eyes into the same blue sky she had been under her entire life and maybe she would recognize it. He saw maybe a father and maybe a daughter sitting at the same table in the same kitchen where he had sat as a teenage boy and he saw them drinking coffee and trying to figure out each other like he and Maryann had done. This stone that had been thrown into his life from some unknown direction and he heard her say it like she had said before. You need me. He saw her helping him clean up the damage he had done to the potter's barn and he saw her walking barefoot in the evening sun. And then he saw himself along a dark road and he saw the wolves that had been lying low in the night and they leaped for him, their sharp teeth snapping at his heels and he saw himself running and trying to get away. And then as the crowd began to chant live or die he saw an open space in the earth and the extended fiery fingers of a flaming hand rising out and reaching for him, charring the nape of his neck.

'Jack,' she yelled. The three hard syllables of live or die

amplified as the voices grew in unison. 'Jack, what are they saying? I know you hear them. Jack!'

She squeezed his fingers and he broke from his trance. Live or die, they chanted. He stepped back from her and turned a slow circle and it came from all sides of the cage. Their thrusting cries and ravenous faces and all the world collapsing upon him as he turned in a circle and felt the weight of his sins. And then Big Momma Sweet raised a cowbell attached to a handle and as he reached out to touch Annette again, Big Momma shook it with vigor and the crowd roared with the clanging and it began.

When he turned Ax was coming toward him with the ferocity of a man who had been born into a rage and never departed from it. The young man charged and did not swing but instead flailed his entire body wildly at Jack as if to simply capture and crush him. Jack ducked away and sank two hard fists into the kidneys and the crowd dove off into hysteria with the first blows. Jack didn't wait because he knew it had to happen quickly if it was going to happen so he drove his heel into the back of the young man's knee. Buckled him. A fist and an elbow into the side of his head and Ax wobbled and fell against the cage. Held himself up and he was bathed in cries of disgust from the crowd as Jack drove a foot into his groin and hit like a hammer and tried to bring him to the ground. Annette stood and clenched the fence and Jack surged with everything available to him as the young man covered himself with one arm and tried to shove Jack away with the other. Behind Annette someone yelled I can't believe this shit. I can't believe I bet on this son of a bitch dying and he's about to straight up goddamn win. She turned around as the man tossed what looked like a carnival ticket to the ground and she knelt and picked up it. Scribbled across the back of the red ticket were an L and a D and the D was circled and it struck her what they meant by live or die.

She pressed her face to the fence and cried out his name, desperate to get his attention and desperate to somehow get him to realize what they were all there for but he could not hear. All his strength went into the opponent. Jack had hurt him and he kept punching against the top of his head and into his gut but the young man would not go down to his knees. Down to his knees where Jack would never let him out of this state of surprise and the next stop after his knees would be the ground and then Jack could drive his fist into his temple over and over until the man either cried no more or lost consciousness and then there would be the clang of the cowbell. The crowd booed as the muscled young man covered himself and used the cage to stay upright and Jack punched and kicked and elbowed, going for the finish. But he could not get around that corner and he had no stamina and he began to slow. Like a windup toy that can only go so far.

He stepped away from Ax. Looked at Annette and she was screaming to him through cupped hands but she was drowned out by the crowd. The sweat ran down his face and dripped from his ears and the young man's blood was scattered across his knuckles. He fought for his breath and lunged toward Ax again but Ax had been waiting for him to run low and he was ready with his bricklike elbow and it caught Jack across the temple. Jack spun and dropped to his hands and knees. An instant shrill pitch ringing in his head and the dirt floor spinning and the cries of the crowd muffled. He squeezed his own forehead with both hands and tried to get his eyes to settle. Tried to squeeze out the ringing. Knew he had to get up and get away but then he felt the large hand wrapping the back of his neck and Ax lifted him to his feet as if he were no more than a puppet without a string.

And the fight was over. His brain ablaze and his vision in

circles and he had nothing left to give. With each passing blow to the face or to the head, with each knee into his back and clutch of his throat he had less and less energy to defend himself and it turned into a demonstration of punishment. The young and strong versus the tired and dying. Ax lifted and slammed Jack flat on his back against the trampled dirt, the thud so pronounced that it tempered the crowd for half a second until it could roar again for more. Jack was lifted and thrown against the cage. Face into the chainlinks. Slammed into the posts. Picked up and thrown sideways. The skin of his chest and arms catching and ripping on the jagged bits of the cage. A bloody ragdoll who did not know where he was but only that the end was coming and his eyes filled with dirt and blood.

The young man stalked and teased and he was going to make them all remember the final time they laid eyes on Jack Boucher with this lasting exhibition of brutality. He played to the crowd as he taunted and allowed Jack to get to his feet. Jack staggered blindly, reaching his hands out as if he were a child only beginning to walk, hoping for a larger, loving hand to take hold and lead his way. The crowd howled and laughed. All but one. And she sat in the corner, pleading for him to get away. Not to get away so that he may find a way to win but only to get away so that he may live, watching between her fingers as the young man mocked Jack's dumb and damaged gait as if they were actors in some morbid vaudeville. And after several steps the young man measured him again and sank his fist into an already broken face. The crowd gasping each time Jack went to the ground. Amazed each time he somehow rose again.

And then in a brief moment of respite, as the crowd was catching its breath. As Jack lay on his stomach and face and moved when no one thought he would move again. As Annette went down to her knees and begged for it all to stop. In that moment of respite a voice from somewhere in the depths of the crowd cried out a single word that all could hear.

Mercy.

There was a pause of disbelief.

And then another voice joined.

Mercy.

Big Momma Sweet stood. Three and four more calls for mercy and then a dozen more in quick succession and she raised the shotgun and there was silence. But before she could speak the voices of the bloodthirsty attacked the voices of mercy. First drowning them out with threats and then putting the threats into action and fists began to fly among the crowd. Those who had called for mercy versus those who wanted none of it and around the cage the crowd swayed and wrestled against itself in a wave of primal chaos.

Annette stayed on her knees and called for Jack. Dug her fingers into the dirt and prayed in frantic shouts for a God to come and save him. Some God. Any God. Get him away from this nightmare. Her voice only a whimper against the surrounding violence and the ears of benevolence far away from this place. Ax began to amble across the floor of the cage. Dumbfounded by the mob of bodies and the way in which the melee seemed to feed on its own energy and not a man outside the cage remained unengaged. It was hit or be hit. Ax looked up at Big Momma Sweet who seemed neither concerned nor entertained as she watched the carnage. The shotgun propped on her shoulder. Ern stood beneath her with the billy club in one hand and the searing iron in the other as the crowd grabbed and struck and tumbled.

What no one but Annette noticed was Jack beginning to crawl. A bloodied and wounded worm working its way across the hardened earth. Working on his elbows. One after another in small increments, making his way toward the corner of the cage. His face in shades of red and his body numb with the pain and his consciousness drifting into a place free and clear of it all. He crept on undetected and he made it into the corner. Put his fingers into the fence and pulled himself to his knees and he took a finger and wiped the blood and grime from his eyes. When he looked up again he did not see the crazed crowd or the bright white lights hanging from the steel beams. He did not hear the voices of hostility or the prayers from Annette.

He saw her again. The same peaceful face and winding white hair that had been there to help him from the wreck. Pensive, motherly eyes. And the sweet voice meant only for him.

On the ground, she said. On the ground right next to you. Only look down and you will see it. Your pants have ripped and it has fallen out and look at it on the ground. It is beside your knee. No one is looking so pick it up. They are too busy with themselves.

Her figure ghostly and her white hair swaying and slinking through the chainlinks and he felt her hand across the back of his head as he looked down to the ground. Her voice serene and steady and telling him it is right there beside you. Pick it up. He wiped at his eyes again and his vision clouded but he thought he saw it. Right beside his knee like she said. The four humps of his brass knuckles.

Go ahead, Jack. Pick it up. It's okay. No one is watching but don't wait any longer. Pick it up and slide it on your hand.

He did.

Now, she said. Catch your breath. He is coming. And I will see you again soon. And she will be there with us. She is waiting like I am for you to slide it on your hand and finish this. She is the only one watching you and she will take you out of here when it is over. You know what to do. He is coming.

Bring me home.

He lifted his hand to touch her face but she was a fading apparition and then gone. He then looked at the brass knuckles across the fingers of his right hand. The scarred, bloodied right hand. And then he sucked in a big breath and closed his eyes and in the caverns of his eroding soul he searched for every fragment of hate and resentment and the fragments came with sharp edges. He found the rughaired boy and the blank faces of a woman and a man who emptied him into this world and he found the anxiety of abandonment and the black hours of childhood loneliness and the desolation of the unknown. He found the fanged faces of addiction that had lived with him in the musty rooms and he found the long and lasting losing streaks where he flushed away the work of generations for the sake of simple, selfish thrills. He found the self-loathing that he did not have the guts to rail against and he found his own drugged eyes looking back at him in the mirror of disgrace. He conjured all the hate and all the regret into one single fit of rage and when the young man reached to grab him again by the back of the neck, the fighter rose and spun around and delivered the brass knuckles to the space between the eyes with one final fist of fury.

There was a crack. A suspension of the moment as the young man waited for gravity to decide in which direction his muscular body would fall. And then as he collapsed to the ground a shotgun blast blew a hole in the metal roof and interrupted the carnage. The crowd ducked in unison with the blast and then one by one they let go of one another. Pulled one another to their feet. Looked to Big Momma Sweet who was holding the shotgun tilted down into the cage, a ribbon of smoke curling from the barrel.

And with a stunned silence they looked upon the grotesque figure of Jack Boucher. Standing over the body of the motionless giant. The blood and sweat covering Jack's body and dripping from his nose and chin. A puddle of salvation forming in the dirt between his feet.

EPILOGUE

'*I wish I knew who I was,*' *he said to her one evening. A lavender dusk and the last smooth band of sunlight drawn across the horizon.*

He didn't know where the words came from and after it was said he looked around as if they had been spoken by a third among them. Maryann stopped rocking and she crossed her hands in her lap. He turned his head away from her and hoped that maybe she hadn't heard what he said. He had turned nineteen only months before and finished high school only weeks before. A packed duffel bag sat next to the closet door in his bedroom and in a few days' time he would leave and drive to Texas. Follow the fighting circuit back across the South. Try to make a name for himself. The beginning of a cycle that would not end. He had been talking about it since he turned eighteen and she had tried to dissuade him. Tried to talk him into finding another life. One without the risks. But he believed that the risks belonged only to the man standing opposite him and the lure of the road was too strong for his young and searching heart.

A breeze rustled the leaves of the trees and crickets called out into the early night. He stood up and leaned on the porch rail and his hair had grown long and it blew across his eyes.

'*That's something you'll never know,*' *she finally said.*

It was not what he had anticipated. He had said the words that had been rumbling inside of him for his entire life and he had said them to this woman so full of optimism and grace believing she would let them land softly in a cloud of consolation but instead she delivered the blunt and direct. He looked at her. A shadowy and vague figure in this dream time between day and night and her eyes were not on him but still fixed upon that distant world. Then he said I guess not. I already gave up anyhow.

She halfsmiled and said no you haven't given up and there's no reason to. But we always are looking for who we are. You. Me. All of us. And that doesn't have anything to do with your blood. She touched her hand to her chest and said it is in here and then she pointed to her head and said not so much in here. Because you never stop wanting to know who you are and when you think you have it figured out life has a way of tapping you on the shoulder and shifting what you thought you knew.

He stood upright. A long silence between them as they watched the last light of day sink into the earth.

'Life drove up to my house in a white van about seven years ago,' she continued. 'It gave _me_ something strong. It gave something honest and tender and it asked me to become something else and I thought I was ready for it. But I wasn't. And I know I'm different than I was before you came here. And that is what I mean. You will want to know who you are today and tomorrow and the next day for the rest of your life. And that is good, Jack. Some days you will think about it more than other days. It would be sad to me if you didn't think about it at all.'

He walked to the far end of the porch and back again. Sat down in the rocker.

'What do you see way out there?' he asked.

'It depends,' she said.

'On what?'

'I'm not exactly sure.'

'So what do you see out there?' he asked again.

The wind died down and the earth seemed to pause while waiting on her to answer. Jack stood and folded his arms and leaned against the porch column. A wild screech pealed across the land and the first stars appeared in the crown of the sky. I see it too, he wanted to say. Whatever it is that you see I think I can see it too. He wanted to tell her that but he wanted more to hear what she would say, so he kept quiet. He leaned in the dark and waited for her words to come like some prayer that he would always remember. I see it too, he thought. Way out there.

She stood and walked over to him. She took his hand and raised it with hers and together they pointed into the distance, out toward this cobalt canvas of questions and then she lowered their arms and they stood together in the gulf of night as if waiting for something impossible to happen. And then she opened her lips and whispered. I don't know what I see, she said. That's why I keep looking.

ACKNOWLEDGMENTS

My thanks go to Ellen Levine and the team at Trident Media Group. To Lee Boudreaux, Carrie Neill, and all the hardworking crew at Lee Boudreaux Books and Little, Brown. To Jason Richman and Yuli Masinovsky. To No Exit Press and Sonatine Editions. To the Mississippi Arts Commission for its financial support. To my friend Bryan Hilliard. And most of all to my little fighters, Brooklyn and Presley, and to Sabrea, the toughest gal on the block.